INSPECTOR GHOTE PLAYS A JOKER

INSPECTOR GHOTE PLAYS A JOKER

H. R. F. Keating

CHIVERS
THORNDIKE

This Large Print book is published by BBC Audiobooks Ltd, Bath, England and by Thorndike Press®, Waterville, Maine, USA.

Published in 2005 in the U.K. by arrangement with the author.

Published in 2005 in the U.S. by arrangement with The Peters Fraser Dunlop Group Ltd.

U.K. Hardcover ISBN 1–4056–3264–X (Chivers Large Print)
U.K. Softcover ISBN 1–4056–3265–8 (Camden Large Print)
U.S. Softcover ISBN 0–7862–7427–1 (Nightingale)

The text of this Large Print edition is unabridged.
Other aspects of the book may vary from the original edition.

Set in 16 pt. New Times Roman.

Printed in Great Britain on acid-free paper.

British Library Cataloguing in Publication Data available

Library of Congress Cataloging-in-Publication Data

Keating, H. R. F. (Henry Raymond Fitzwalter), 1926–
　　Inspector Ghote plays a joker / by H.R.F. Keating.
　　　　p.　　cm. — (Thorndike Press large print Nightingale)
　　ISBN 0–7862–7427–1 (lg. print : sc : alk. paper)
　　1. Ghote, Ganesh (Fictitious character)—Fiction. 2. Police—India—Bombay—Fiction. 3. Bombay (India)—Fiction.
　　4. Large type books. I. Title. II. Series.
　　PR6061.E26I4 2005
　　823'.914—dc22　　　　　　　　　　　　　　　　　2004030172

1

Inspector Ganesh Ghote stood too stiffly at attention in front of Deputy Superintendent Naik's desk in the Bombay C.I.D. headquarters. The Deputy Superintendent was considering a letter. It seemed to be causing him some trouble. It was not long, Ghote could see. Two short typed paragraphs on a single broad sheet of official notepaper. But it evidently posed considerable problems, to judge by the way D.S.P. Naik was simply staring at it puffing laboriously through his rather protuberant lips under the soft blur of his moustache.

At last he looked up.

'Ah, Ghote,' he said. 'Good.'

Ghote tried rapidly to decide what exact inflection he had heard given to the word 'good.' Had it been said in a way that indicated the D.S.P. was genuinely glad to have him here? Or, had the overtones of pleasure he thought he had detected merely been indications that the D.S.P. was pleased that the lamb had come to the slaughter juicy and well-fed?

There was a glint in the dark brown eyes that looked up at him. That was certain. There was an odd look in the round face which normally was either quite expressionless or wildly choking in a sudden outburst of rage. It looked as if the butcher was about to swing his cleaver.

Ghote straightened his thin shoulders to receive the blow.

'Inspector,' the D.S.P. said, 'I want you to stop a murder.'

'Yes, sir.'

The D.S.P. looked up at him steadily.

After a long silence he spoke again.

'Well, man, no comment?'

'Comment, D.S.P.?'

'I suppose it's not every day you're asked to stop a murder, Inspector?'

'No, sir. No.'

Ghote realised that more was required.

'It is most unusual, sir,' he said.

'Good. So then . . . ?'

Ghote experienced an odd sense of events failing to take their usual course in some way which he was unable to account for. As far as he could make out he was being given instructions on a new case. D.S.P. Naik had summoned him for this purpose before times without number, and the procedure was invariable. He would knock on the office door, wait to hear the barked word 'Come,' enter, stand to attention in front of the desk till the D.S.P. was ready and then listen hard while a stream of new facts was poured out in front of him. If D.S.P. Naik was open to criticism, it might be said he tended to go into too much detail.

But now there was this silence, these silences.

With a definite sense of relief Ghote noticed a familiar symptom beginning to manifest itself on the Deputy Superintendent's rounded features. The blood was coming pounding up into his cheeks, turning the pale brown smooth skin several shades darker. He was brewing up into one of his rages.

'Ask, man, ask,' the D.S.P. suddenly snapped. 'If I say you are to stop a murder, Inspector, haven't you the simple gumption to ask whose murder you are to stop?'

'Yes, sir. No, sir.'

Ghote recovered himself triumphantly.

'Whose murder am I to stop, D.S.P. sahib?' he asked.

D.S.P. Naik leant very slowly back in his wooden armchair while the rage-blood slowly ebbed from his podgy cheeks. When he had leant as far back as he could, he looked Ghote blandly in the face and answered his question.

'You are to stop the murder of a flamingo, Inspector.'

'Yes, sir.'

D.S.P. Naik bounced up as he sat. The blood began to swoosh into his cheeks again.

'Yes, sir,' he mimicked. 'Yes, sir. All you can say is "Yes, sir" when—Oh, never mind.'

The rage drained out of him and he slumped his elbows heavily forward on the dark-brown, leather-covered desk top in front of him.

And then Ghote realised that the D.S.P. had been attempting a joke. There could be no doubt about it. It might never have happened before: the D.S.P. was a serious man. But there could be no getting past it now: he had definitely been trying to make a joke. And it had been allowed to fall absolutely flat.

Would a smile of farewell for it be in order? No, it was too late even for that.

But this new silence could not be allowed to last any longer.

'You were saying, D.S.P. sahib?' Ghote ventured.

'A flamingo, Inspector,' D.S.P. Naik said dully. 'I have here a letter pointing out to me that during the past week three of the four new Red Flamingoes in the zoo in Victoria Gardens have been shot.'

'Oh, yes, sir,' Ghote broke in, snatching the chance to show he was not slow about everything. 'I have seen that in the paper, sir.'

'Have you, Inspector?' D.S.P. Naik said, without showing much appreciation. 'And did you see where the flamingoes came from?'

'Came from, sir? But from some swamp— Oh, no, sir. I remember now. They are a special sort of flamingo, sir. They come from America. Gift of the U.S. Consul, sir.'

Ghote felt a moderate pride at having remembered all these details from a bottom-of-the-column story in the paper two days

4

before.

'A gift of the U.S. Consul,' D.S.P. Naik noted. 'A gift who to, Inspector?'

Ghote racked his brains. Obviously the gift must not have been to the Zoological Gardens themselves or the D.S.P. would not have made a point of asking. Then—Yes. Got it.

'It was a gift to the State Government, sir.'

'I am glad to find my officers can devote so much time to newspaper reading.'

But the D.S.P. did not seem actually furious about this. There was plainly something more to come.

'And which Minister in the State Government would have responsibility for such a gift, Inspector?'

Ghote gave up.

'Cannot say, D.S.P.'

'It is the Minister for Police Affairs and the Arts, Inspector,' D.S.P. Naik replied, with the bitterness only just being held in check. 'The Minister for Police Affairs and the Arts, the New Minister for Police Affairs and the Arts, the Minister who has publicly pledged himself to step up the efficiency and good order of police work in Bombay, Inspector. And, Inspector, he has specifically mentioned your name as the officer he wishes to prevent any further outbreaks of irresponsible hooliganism at the zoo.'

'My name, D.S.P. ?'

'Yours, Inspector. Don't ask me why. He

says he had been given your name as an officer of great resource and particularly requests that you shall handle the case.'

'Yes, D.S.P.'

'Very well, Inspector. There is still one more Red Flamingo left up there at the zoo. Please see that it is in no circumstances murdered.'

'Very good, D.S.P. sahib.'

It sounded as if the interview was over. He turned smartly on his heel. But the D.S.P.'s cup of bitterness had a few dregs left.

'And, Inspector.'

'Yes, D.S.P. ?'

'Do not hesitate to call for any men you want from an already over-worked and persistently underpaid police force.'

'No, sir.'

'Here they are, Inspector. Or, rather I should say, there it is.'

The elderly little man in the Director's Office at Bombay's Victoria Gardens Zoo heaved on the thin cord which controlled the cane blind over the main window. Slowly and jerkily the blind went up to about two-thirds of its height and outside in the strong sunlight Inspector Ghote saw the sole Red Flamingo remaining out of the gift of four from the American Consul.

It was standing on long thin bright pink legs, beautiful but sad, near the edge of a small shallow concrete pond in which a few clumps of coarse reeds grew. The sun brought up the touch of pale pink in the white of its rounded back and just caught the astonished red under one of its wings as it stretched it down till its tip touched the muddy water at its feet in a gesture of profound boredom. Its long bendy neck twisted to carry its little head with the broad hooked pink beak round to survey the comparatively narrow confines of its present and lonely home.

This was a circular cage about fifteen yards across, most of which was taken up by the round pool. The cage was open at the top but its sides, which were of a fairly close-meshed wire, were a good eight feet high. Round them a small crowd stood, students in couples with nothing better to do, and children accompanied either by somewhat indifferent mothers or by even more noticeably unconcerned ayahs. Apparently the general public were not expecting another outbreak of shooting. But then, if Ghote's memory served him, only one flamingo death, the second, had been reported in the papers and that briefly.

He turned to his companion, still holding with both hands firmly on to the thin blind-cord as if, were he to let it go, some appallingly heavy object would descend on both their heads.

'Tell me,' Ghote said, 'have you nowhere else you can put the bird? It does not seem to me entirely safe from a determined killer out there.'

The acting-Director of the Zoological Gardens shook his head in an emphatic flurry of disclaimer.

'It is not safe,' he said. 'Not safe at all. If I had my way that animal, which after all is valued somewhere in the neighbourhood of Rupees three thousand, would be most stringently kept from the public gaze.'

'And why is it not?' Ghote asked.

The acting-Director's small, triangular-cheeked face assumed an expression of great personal pain.

'It is on the direct insistence of the Minister,' he said. 'I received a personal telephone call from a gentleman I understand to be his Public Relations Officer, a Mr Kamdar. He instructed me that the Minister regards these incidents as a challenge. He suspects there are political overtones. He wishes the remaining birds to stay where they can be plainly seen. The gentleman was most emphatic.'

He turned, still holding the blind-cord, and looked at the telephone on the big, old shiny desk in the middle of the cool, shaded room as if he was still hearing the barked commands that had come from it.

Ghote, his heart at the mention of political overtones sinking even farther than it had done already, also stood looking at the big desk in silence. He had found the acting-Director sitting at it when he had been

8

ushered in a few minutes before, sitting not at the high-backed, heavy, cane-seated arm-chair that was ranged squarely in front of the desk knee-hole, but at a small round-backed bentwood chair which he had drawn up uncomfortably to one side. Evidently he was a man determined to make his position clear: he was not the Director, he was no more than acting-Director, and nor did he mean to be anything else.

Resolutely Ghote thrust out of his mind those incidental words about political overtones. If he was going to get enmeshed in the activities of anti-American hotheads, then he was. But at the moment what he wanted was a few simple facts.

'Very well,' he said, 'if the bird is to remain out there, it is to remain out there. But was that where the other ones were when they were shot?'

'It was, exactly,' replied the acting-Director, turning back to give the brightly sunlit scene outside an intent look.

'And when did the first incident take place?'

Ghote pulled a notebook from his pocket. Details, and as many of them as possible, were what he wanted now.

The acting-Director swivelled round on the taut blind-cord.

'It was ten days ago,' he said. 'At much about this time of day, the late afternoon. Perhaps about twenty minutes before the

9

public were due to leave the gardens.'

Something in his tone indicated that the departure of the public from the neighbourhood of the zoo was the high spot of his day.

'And what exactly happened?' Ghote asked methodically.

'That of course I cannot say. The Director was here himself at that time. I understand that the bird fell down, and that after a while one of the keepers noticed and entered the cage to effect an inspection. He found that the animal was dead.'

'I see. And the second case?'

'That was four days later. By then the Director had left for Nepal where he is undertaking some business for the zoo. I was in here. As a matter of fact, I happened to be looking out of the window just as I am now.'

The acting-Director gave a small hitch to the blind-cord which must, Ghote thought, have been cutting into the palm of his hand in a decidedly painful manner for quite some time now.

'Good,' Ghote said encouragingly. 'Then you were an eye-witness to the incident.'

'Yes, yes. I saw the bird fall. It gave a slight jump in a wholly uncharacteristic manner and then it toppled—yes, I think that would be the word—it toppled down on to its side. I left the office at once, you understand, and hurried to the pool. The bird was quite dead. It had been

10

shot through the heart.'

'And there was no sign of any person bearing a gun?'

'None at all. None at all. The shot quite clearly came from a considerable distance.'

The acting-Director drew his small mouth suddenly together as if he had just bitten into a lemon.

'It was then that I decided to inform the Minister,' he said. 'And of course, the Director—by telegram. I fear, however, that the Director did not altogether agree with my action.'

He sighed.

'He has since told me by telephone he has no intention of returning from Nepal until the whole affair is cleared up,' he said.

Ghote decided it would be a kindness to return briskly to details.

'And the third case occurred yesterday?' he said sharply.

'Yes, and again at the same time. Only on this occasion I was not able to witness the occurrence. However, our Deputy Head Keeper (Avians and Small Reptiles) happened to be on the spot, and he reported that the bird was also killed by a shot in the heart.'

. . . *and Small R*, Ghote scribbled in his notebook.

'Yes,' he said. 'I shall have to see that man to get a full report. But one thing struck me. You say both birds were shot through the

11

heart?'

'All three were, as subsequent post-mortem examination has confirmed.'

'But this implies that a bullet was fired. It was not a shotgun matter?'

'No, no. The birds were killed by a rifleman. Quite definitely. They tell me that it was a weapon of small calibre.'

'But the marksman might have operated at some distance?' Ghote asked.

'Oh yes. Oh yes. Look.'

The acting-Director pointed with one free hand through the bright oblong of the window beside him.

'We are very much surrounded by the city here, as you know,' he said. 'It is a location by no means suitable for a properly conducted zoological establishment. So you see, up there: mill buildings of various sorts. Anyone on the roofs of any of those places could shoot down into the gardens. Anyone at all. Or they could shoot from the main body of the Victoria Gardens. From anywhere.'

Ghote sensed a great cloud of heavy despondency hovering over him. But he made up his mind that he would fight it off.

'Very well,' he said briskly. 'For the time being we will abandon the approach by opportunity, and we will tackle the approach by motive. Would you be good enough to obtain for me a list of any personnel recently dismissed?'

12

'There is no one.'

'No one? But surely—'

'Three years ago we dismissed an assistant keeper. There was a strike. The animals suffered severely. It is now not our policy to effect dismissals.'

'I see,' said Ghote.

He carefully turned to the other end of the scale and flipped to a new page in his notebook.

'Well, can you outline for me the offices and duties of the senior staff here?' he asked.

If it was impossible to dismiss a lowly assistant keeper, it was certainly possible to remove a Director who had allowed valuable birds to be shot. And with the Director dismissed an attractive vacancy would be there for the filling.

'Yes, senior posts are a very simple matter,' the acting-Director replied. 'We are not a large organisation, disgracefully small in fact. But other branches of science appear to receive priority.'

'So there are how many senior posts?' Ghote asked quickly.

'There is the Director, who, naturally, has a deputy. And then there is only myself, my official title is Head of Research, and I am at present, as you know, acting-Director.'

The acting-Director turned from the window and looked with confidence at the arrangement of chairs at the big desk. He had

13

defined his position, and was proud of it.

'And the Director is in Nepal, you say?' Ghote asked.

'Yes. It is his life ambition to secure a Yeti for the zoo. He considers the so-called Abominable Snowman would be a public attraction. And so even though his retirement date is a good many years away, he frequently visits Nepal.'

'I see,' Ghote said.

His suspicions were sharpening by the second with the information about the Director's long future tenure of his job.

'But you, you say, are only acting-Director,' he went on. 'There is a Deputy Director also. Where is he?'

Pretending to be on holiday, no doubt. And lurking round with a small calibre rifle.

'Dead,' said the acting-Director.

'Dead?'

The acting-Director bowed his small, worried head.

'Yes,' he said. 'A coronary thrombosis, poor fellow. He went quite suddenly less than six months ago. That is why we are so much at sixes and sevens, to tell you the truth.'

'No arrangements have been made to replace him?' Ghote asked. 'No junior staff have been promoted?'

'There is only the Head Keeper and Deputy Heads, and they are quite unqualified scientifically.'

14

The acting-Director sighed deeply.

'Ever since poor Karandikar died things have been appalling,' he said. 'Sometimes I think I would be better dead myself. I think we would all be better dead.'

Ghote felt that this onset of black pessimism deserved at least some passing tribute.

'Very true, very true,' he remarked. 'There are times when one feels we would all be better dead.'

He stood for a respectful moment staring through the bright oblong of the window.

And suddenly the elegant long-legged bird in the circular wire enclosure jumped about a foot into the air in a flurry of abruptly ungainly feathers and then flopped over sideways on to the concrete edge of its pond. For two seconds Ghote stared at it unbelievingly. But then a faint sound that he had heard superimposed over the throbbing noise of city life slipped into place in his mind.

'Shot,' he said. 'That bird has been shot.'

2

It took Ghote barely a minute to run out of the zoo Director's office, through an outer room clacking with typewriter noises, out into the main hall of the Administrative Building, down a broad flight of stone steps, round two corners and across to the circular wire-fenced pond where now the last remaining Red Flamingo of the American Consul's gift lay patently dead.

It took the zoo's acting-Director rather longer to follow the same course, and even longer to send a young assistant-keeper back to the office to fetch the key of the flamingo cage. However, even allowing for the acting-Director's painful, slow selection of the right key from a large numbered bunch, it was within three minutes of the shooting that Ghote was crouching beside the body of the victim.

'Yes,' he said. 'Right in the centre of the breast, just like the others. This fellow we are up against must be a pretty fine shot.'

The acting-Director, who had been standing at the edge of the pond peering over at the body of his dead charge, stepped hastily back and gave an anxious look round. He patted at his wrinkled, triangular cheeks.

'Well,' he said cautiously, 'at least it is hardly likely to be anyone directly connected with the Zoological Gardens: none of our keepers is likely to be an experienced rifleman.'

'No, I think you can rest assured . . .' Ghote murmured.

His mind was busy elsewhere. He looked all round and then stepped boldly into the shallow pool up to his knees. With care he

16

stationed himself as close as he could recollect to the exact spot at which the flamingo had been standing at the moment of its death. He faced in the direction to which the bird had presented its faintly pink-tinged white breast. He looked up.

The Victoria and Albert Museum. That hundred-year-old solid building, part of Britain's heavy legacy to Bombay, fell squarely into his line of view. But something else was even more accurately in line. Just above the square-looking block of the museum he could see the thin tip of the clock tower built in front of it. That would be an ideal place. Perhaps even at this instant the marksman was looking at him from its vantage-point.

'Come on,' he shouted.

In two strides he waded out of the pond. He raced, dripping, out of the wide open door of the circular cage. He turned and set off at a purposeful lope through the surrounding zoo. Out of the corners of his eyes he glimpsed cages of monkeys, swinging, gibbering or huddled scratching; there was a tiger prowling rapidly across a small thickly-barred cage; the hot sun was bringing up the sharp smell of penned beasts; mothers and ayahs hereabouts were more anxious over their charges than they had been back beside the peaceful-looking flamingo, the sound of women scolding trailed across the back of his mind as he ran.

At the exit turnstile he was held up for a few moments while a large family party filed through ahead of him—tense-faced father in loose white shirt and baggy white trousers, two boys in neat shorts and still clean, white shirts, an older sister wearing a dark blue blouse and a blue and white striped cotton skirt, her hair in long braids, and the mother in a fierce yellow sari bringing up the rear looking sharply from side to side through big spectacles making sure they had missed not an anna's worth of pleasure from the visit before they finally left.

And then at a faster lope through the Victoria Gardens themselves, his sodden trouser-bottoms batting regularly against his shins now, clammily uncomfortable.

He had been here only once in recent years, bringing his little son on a not altogether successful expedition to see the great rock-carved elephant that had once stood on the Island of Elephanta out in the harbour. Its crumbling surface had interested him himself, with its half-told story of all that it had witnessed over so many years, but it had left little Ved totally unimpressed. But at least he remembered from that visit the general lay-out of the gardens and it was easy enough to take the quickest route through them past neat flower-beds and heavy shrubberies to the museum near the west entrance and the clock tower beyond it.

Running steadily along the gravelled asphalt paths, swinging past the strolling visitors, he even had time to notice, with dismay, the number of people who could conceivably be carrying a concealed rifle. There was a naked-chested mali stooping under a great bundle of long sticks whom he almost stopped and demanded to search, only it was unlikely that someone who looked so like a gardener would be the sort of person to shoot with a sporting rifle. A beggar with a crutch was even more unlikely, but always possible. But that serious-faced young man marching solemnly along with a folded raincoat drooping low over his arm . . .

But no. Better to take the chance that the fellow was still in the clock tower. He would after all want to observe the havoc his shot had caused. That would be the point of the joke, if joker it was: to see the quickly gathering crowd round the body of the dead bird, the hurried comings and goings, the confusion. It was very likely the fellow was still up in the top of the tower there, probably with a pair of binoculars if he was the sort who was used to a sporting rifle.

The heavy bulk of the Victoria and Albert Museum loomed up in front of him. He swung to the left and ran round.

And there was the clock tower, slim and tall. There was a scattering of people in front of the museum, mostly children with mothers or fathers, but no one in the immediate vicinity of the tower. Was his man still up there?

He walked quickly across to the tower's base. There on the far side was a narrow, low metal door painted a dull red and with a line of heavy rivet-heads running across its middle. There was a large key-hole on the right-hand side.

Ghote put out a hand and pushed at the door. It moved back at his touch. So it looked as if he was right: someone had succeeded in unlocking the door that should have been shut firm. But had he himself been quick enough to have outsmarted the man behind the rifle?

He thought for a moment, and then he hooked a finger in the key-hole and drew the door closed again before moving across and stationing himself where anyone coming out would be screened from him by the opening door. He waited patiently. The declining sun was still strong enough to dry off the bottoms of his trousers and his squelchy shoes.

Across at the entrance to the museum people began streaming out in a thickening crowd. The attendants inside must be going round saying that closing-time was near. Had his marksman taken note of this daily event, and did he intend to mingle with the people hurrying past on their way out? There were enough of them now to make it easy for anyone wishing to melt out of sight before anybody started asking questions about why

20

they had been in the clock tower.

But the dull red iron door stayed unmoving. Eventually the acting-Director came round the corner of the museum with three excited, chattering keepers following him. He looked like a man doing his duty, unpleasant though it was.

Ghote stepped out from the wall of the tower.

'Over here,' he called.

The acting-Director and his posse came up.

'I am almost certain that the shooting took place in the tower here,' Ghote said. 'And it is just possible the culprit is still up there. I am going to look now. Will you station your men at this door, please? It is possible the fellow may be too strong for me.'

The acting-Director looked as if he had just been told an extremely improper story.

'Would it not be better to send for the police?' he asked.

'I am the police,' Ghote said.

He turned and pushed at the little reddish door. It moved slowly at his touch.

Directly in front of him was an extremely narrow spiral iron-work staircase, winding up round a slender central pillar. It was very dark inside, with only a faint patch of light coming from a narrow vertical slit in the tower walls perhaps ten or twelve feet up. Very quietly Ghote began to ascend.

It took a long time. The stairs wound round

21

and round with dim areas of light from the short slits cut every ten feet or so into the walls, now on one side now on another. At the darkest point between each Ghote waited where he could least be seen and stood listening intently. From about two-thirds of the way up he began to hear the working of the machinery of the big clock up above him, a steady, heavy echoing tock. But strain as he might he could not detect any other sound.

As he approached the top the light grew stronger. Looking up, he was able to make out that it flooded in evenly from each side of the tower, but it was still muted and no doubt the apertures through which it came were not large. And then he became aware of something new, an extra odour superimposed on the dank smell that seemed to come from the cool ironwork. It was the scent of tobacco smoke.

He crept a few steps higher and delicately sniffed again. Yes, tobacco. Someone had been smoking a cigarette up here and very recently too. Nor was it some rank leaf-rolled bidi. It was a cigarette of quality. Such as you might expect the possessor of a fine sporting rifle to smoke.

Ghote strained his ears to catch even a lightly drawn breath.

But there was nothing.

Step by step, inch by inch he moved on up the cool iron stairway. And at last his head was level with the top-most step. He waited.

He had no doubt that in his climb he had made a certain amount of noise, for all the care he had taken. Had someone up in the clock-winding chamber heard him? Were they waiting in absolute quiet for him now? And what about the sporting rifle? Was it even now aimed at the stairhead?

He counted to ten, and then very quietly and easily he raised his head above the level of the top step.

The little clock-winding chamber and the enormous works of the clock itself were all visible to him at his first glance. And they were entirely deserted.

He clambered noisily up the last few steps and stood crouching in the low chamber at the top. He saw now that the light came in through narrow horizontal louvres running all round the top of the tower above the level of the clock. And he found it was easy enough, though a little uncomfortable, to look through them.

From the one facing east he got at once an excellent view of the zoo and of the circular shape of the flamingo pond. There was a fairly large crowd of people gathered round it still, perhaps as many as thirty people. The man who had shot the bird would have enjoyed watching them. Even with the naked eye it was possible to sense the excitement and confusion. People were gesticulating and pointing to the white body of the dead bird; messengers were hurrying away and breathlessly arriving. The joke, extravagant though it was, had been altogether successful.

A gleam of copper at his feet attracted his attention. He stooped. It was a cartridge case. He would have thought a .22. The team from the laboratories would have to come up and collect it and see what they could do about fingerprints. But he doubted if he was going to catch his man that way. This fellow was hardly the sort who would figure in the records, and a .22 bullet cartridge would not tell them very much until they had found the gun that had fired it.

He looked carefully round for a cigarette butt, though that would scarcely be more helpful. There was nothing. The man must have left the tower still smoking, a cool customer. And already the smell of that cigarette was fading away.

Ghote felt that he was losing the last tantalising connection with the joker who had killed the Minister's flamingoes. Would he ever get this near him again?

*   *   *

During the rest of that day he had got no closer to any hint of the elusive personality of the joker, and eventually he had given up and gone home, bad-tempered and dispirited. But

24

next morning he made a point of arriving at Headquarters good and early, just on half past seven, so that he could sit in undisturbed solitude and go over all the possibilities with a fresh mind and with the sage advice of his treasured copy of Hans Gross's 'Criminal Investigation' to hand. If he tackled every angle that arose in a systematic way, some lead worth pursuing would certainly turn up. It had to.

He opened the door of his office with feelings of pleasurable anticipation bubbling quietly inside him.

And the little room was not empty and awaiting him. Sitting on the corner of the desk, his desk, was Sgt. Desai. Ghote looked at him in fury. Sgt. Desai was an error. He was an error on the part of someone who had allowed him into the C.I.D., and Ghote sometimes wondered how on earth they had made it since his complete lack of talent had come bursting to light within days of his arrival. He had been in every department in the building, briefly: the Fingerprint Bureau, Records, Administration, each in turn had eventually sworn they would not have him back. He was certainly not going to moon about in here.

'Good morning, Sergeant,' Ghote said briskly. 'And now, if you do not mind, I have got work to do.'

Sgt. Desai—eyes round in his dark-skinned, smudgy-nosed face—jumped hastily off

25

the desk.

'Good morning, Inspector,' he said. 'A very good morning, sir.'

A wide undirected grin slowly spread across the lower half of his face, showing big, very white teeth. He made no attempt to leave.

'Work,' said Ghote sharply. 'There's work to be done.'

'Yes, Inspector. Right away, Inspector. Anything you want.'

Ghote looked at him sharply. The dunderhead.

'I want you to go,' he said. 'To leave me in peace.'

'But no, Inspector. I can't.'

'Can't? What do you mean "Can't"?'

'I'm allocuted to you, Inspector. D.S.P. Naik allocuted me.'

Ghote felt as if a bucket of cold water had been thrown in his face.

'Allotted to me? By D.S.P. Naik?'

Desai's grin broadened even further.

'That's right, Inspector. Help you on your new case.'

Ghote stood and looked at him. A great burning feeling of rage coloured to brilliant orange everything in his mind.

What on earth did the D.S.P. mean by doing this to him? Saddling him with this fool, the resident idiot, when he had a business of this sort on his hands? The new Minister personally expected results. It was his flamingoes that had been shot. The utmost tact might be required at any moment.

He glanced involuntarily at the phone on his desk. What if it began ringing now and the Minister summoned him? Was Sgt. Desai going to come tagging along too? And stand grinning all over his face throughout the interview?

It was nothing less than criminally irresponsible of the D.S.P. Giving him help on his new case, indeed.

He directed a look of pure fury at the grinning Desai. 'A fat lot of help you will be,' he spat.

And the look of pained astonishment that appeared on Sgt. Desai's simple face at once brought a sharp tongue of regret flicking up at Ghote.

'Well, you had better sit down,' he said, in a less withering tone. 'If the D.S.P. has allocated you to me, we will have to see if there is something you can do.'

In an instant the look of pain on Desai's face was replaced with the slow beginnings of a new grin. He looked carefully round for somewhere to sit, spotted eventually the little heavy wooden chair which was reserved for visitors, backed towards it with his eyes now intent on Ghote and lowered himself down slowly on to its edge.

Resignedly, Ghote set himself to think over the case aloud in front of Desai rather than

27

commit his thoughts to the big pile of scrap paper that he always kept ready in the lowest drawer on the right-hand side of his desk.

'There is one thing clear about this business, Sergeant,' he said, 'and that is that I am not very likely to get anywhere, or rather we are not likely to get anywhere from the point of opportunity to commit the crime. Any single one of a thousand or more people could have slipped into the clock tower in the Victoria Gardens and shot those flamingoes. The key is kept on a hook just inside the Museum, you know. Anybody who kept his eyes open could have got it.'

He looked across at Desai for a reaction. The sergeant was sitting still on the edge of the heavy little chair staring at him intently. His lower lip had drooped a little open. His expression radiated solemn awe. And not a glimmer of anything else.

Ghote resumed his spoken thoughts.

'No help from the science boys last night, of course,' he said, 'and not even enough of a fingerprint on the cartridge I found up in the tower to be of any use, even if we had something to match it against. So we shall just have to consider the business from the point of view of possible motives. Why should anyone want to kill those flamingoes? That is our best bet to go on.'

He thought he saw a trace of liveliness in Desai's wide eyes and stopped to wait for an answer to his question.

Desai leant forward and put his leg relaxedly across the knee of his right.

'Talking of bets, Inspector,' he said, 'I hear Cream of the Jest is a good thing at Mahalaxmi this afternoon.'

Ghote stared at him.

'What did you say?'

'Talking of bets, Inspector, I hear—' the sergeant began again, as if the gramophone needle had been put back exactly the right number of grooves.

'No.'

Ghote brought his open palm slamming down on the scratched surface of the desk in front of him. Sgt. Desai jumped a little but continued to regard him with the same truth-seeking expression.

'We were not talking of bets,' Ghote said. 'We were talking about the killing of the Minister's four flamingoes. I was about to say that there are two possibilities: either it was an act of political demonstration, or it was a simple practical joke. Which of those alternatives do you consider the most likely, Sergeant?'

Desai blinked.

'Well? Which?'

'Could you tell me what the two of them were again, Inspector?'

Ghote drew in a deep breath.

'The birds could have been killed because they were a gift from the American Consul,' he

29

said. 'Or they could have been killed as a mere practical joke. Which do you think most likely?'

For a few moments Ghote sat watching the blind panic on the sergeant's face. He decided he would count very slowly up to ten. But when he had got to eight the sergeant suddenly pounced.

'The second, Inspector,' he gabbled.

'The second?'

'The one you said second, Inspector.'

'And which was that?' Ghote asked.

'Which?'

Desai's question was put in a spirit of pure inquiry. Ghote conscientiously fought down a desire to yell.

'You mean you think it was just a practical joke?' he said.

'Yes, yes, Inspector. Thank you.'

'Well, I think just the opposite,' Ghote countered out of sheer peevishness. 'How could it be just a joke? How could anyone possibly take so much trouble just to make a joke? They could not. It would be a ridiculous waste of time. So we are left with the political angle.'

'Yes, Inspector.'

Desai was back to the awed look.

'I do not much like it, I can tell you,' Ghote said, finding himself now more than half-convinced by his own arguments. 'But I suppose it does have one advantage: it does mean we do not have to deal with all of Bombay's four and a half million inhabitants. We have only got to deal with known anti-Americans. And we can narrow it further too. We know at least one thing for certain about this fellow.'

The spectacle of Desai following this train of thought like a pilgrim plodding out the road to Rishikesh was not helping, but Ghote ploughed on.

'We know that our man is an expert marksman,' he said. 'And if we put these two factors together we really do narrow the field.'

He felt a gleam of excitement. It seemed to infect Desai too, causing him to shift about on the heavy wooden chair.

'That's the point, Inspector,' he said. 'Narrow down the field.'

'Yes,' said Ghote. 'And we must follow it up.'

'Yes, you see, Inspector. The field is narrow for that first race tomorrow. Besides Cream of the Jest there is only one nag that stands a chance, and that's Trencherman. By Digger out of Fat Lady, you know. And you must have heard what they say about Digger as sire.'

'Sergeant!'

'You fancy something each way, Inspector?'

Ghote leant forward across his desk and fixed the sergeant with an unblinking cold gaze.

'I fancy a little concentration on the matter in hand, Sergeant. I was in the middle of

31

explaining that it is possible to narrow down the—It is possible to reduce the number of people who might have committed this crime to a quite small number. Violent anti-Americans who know how to use a .22 rifle with extreme accuracy. There cannot be so many. And I think I know how we can find them. Gunsmiths and shikar outfitters, that will be the way.'

He was pleased with this thought. He looked across at the sergeant. It was plain the sergeant was miles away, up at the Mahalaxmi Racecourse thinking about the going and the handicapping and all the rest of the ridiculously serious factors that obsessed the habitual punter. Well, perhaps he was better lost in daydreams of sudden wealth than interrupting and causing confusion here on the spot.

'Yes,' Ghote resumed. 'This is what we will do: visit the main shikar places, shops like Hunter and Hunter in Altamount Road. You can do half, Sergeant, I will do the other half. Let's start making a list.'

He jerked open the bottom right-hand drawer of the desk and eagerly pulled out half a dozen sheets of scrap. This was it: real progress.

He wrote at the top of the first sheet. Shikar: Hunter and Hunter.

Then he stopped. He had pictured for an instant Sgt. Desai entering that august establishment to which the American millionaires hurried on arrival in Bombay to get themselves properly kitted out for tiger-hunting or teal-shooting. He saw Desai tackling perhaps the manager himself, failing to get to the point, blundering in his English, building up a huge reservoir of indignation. No, it was out of the question. It would be impossible even to go round after him picking up the pieces.

He felt a spasm of renewed irritation. He looked up.

'Listen, Sergeant,' he said, 'go for a walk, get out, run away. I have a lot to do and you are putting me off.'

He might have known it would not be as simple as that. First the sergeant looked at him, taking in what he had said drop by drop. Then he looked pained again. And then he began expostulating.

'But, Inspector, I can't do that. Inspector, I have to be here with you. The D.S.P. sahib said so, Inspector. What would happen if he caught me just sitting about somewhere?'

Ghote gave in.

'Oh, stay then. Stay. We will take a break. Call for some tea. There's a good chap.'

Desai jumped up with alacrity. This was something he understood. He hurried over to the door, just bumping into the bamboo set of shelves on top of which Ghote kept his edition of Gross and slightly altering the position of the sacred volume. Outside he shouted in an altogether unnecessarily noisy way to the peon, and then he marched up and down with maddeningly clumping feet till the tea arrived.

At last Ghote got him back on his chair dangerously balancing his cup and sipping at the tea with, naturally, the maximum of noise.

Wearily Ghote searched about for something to say.

'Tell me, Sergeant, are you married?'

'Oh, yes, Inspector. Yes, I am. Four children, Inspector. Three boys, one girl. No—'

He stopped himself.

'No, I mean three girls, one boy, Inspector.'

He looked pleased to have sorted the matter out.

'You can't help them coming, Inspector,' he said, with an appalling grin, half sly, half self-congratulatory.

Ghote did not reply. But he allowed himself a short inner tirade: Can't help them coming. Lack the damned brains to stop them coming, you mean. It is for people like you they set up Birth Control Centres. Except that people like you would look on the operation as something completely terrifying. Why, oh why, could they not have invented it before you were due to be born, and spared us all ever afterwards?

'And they cost a lot, you know, Inspector. Only you having only the one would not know how much.'

Yes, Ghote thought registering the half-expressed jibe, I could not be expected to know how to multiply by four since obviously the feat would be far beyond you.

But it was time he spoke, and said something that sounded friendly.

'Yes, on a sergeant's pay rate you must find it hard to manage,' he said.

'Bloody hard, Inspector, bloody hard,' Desai replied with a pathetic attempt at a man of the world grin. 'Only one thing for it, man.'

'What is that?' Ghote asked, immediately wishing he had not.

'The horses, Inspector. They are the only thing.'

This is what comes of trying to be friendly, Ghote thought furiously. Back to the idiocies of horse-racing.

Desai was obviously delighted to be back there.

'It is the only way, Inspector,' he went meanderingly on.

'You have to get a red-hot tip and put every anna you can lay your hands on on it.'

He sighed.

'But even then, Inspector, you can come unstuck, you know. Even when you have a horse you know is going to win.'

He cast around for a really impressive example. And surprisingly hit on one almost at once.

'Take the Derby this year, Inspector. Now that was something very unfair, isn't it?'

'Was it?' Ghote asked, taking a long cooling drink of tea.

'But, Inspector.'

Desai sounded genuinely shocked.

'But, Inspector, even you must know about that.'

Even you. The idiot lacked the sense even to show a little tact to the man he was supposed to be working for.

'Know about what, Sergeant?' he asked, no longer able to keep the irritation out of his voice again.

'About Roadside Romeo, the odds-on favourite that disappeared on the morning of the race and they found a donkey in its stable, Inspector.'

Ghote banged down his cup.

'What did you say?'

'. . . morning of the race and they found a donkey in its stable, Inspector,' Desai repeated in his gramophone way.

'And this was the Derby this year?'

'Yes, Inspector.'

'When is that?'

'When is what, Inspector?'

'The Derby. The Derby, you fool.'

'But everybody knows that, Inspector.'

'I do not. When was it? Quick.'

'It was—let me see—Funny the way I forget things.'

Ghote clenched his fist.

'January the twenty-ninth, Inspector. I knew

36

I would remember sooner or later.'

'Just under three months ago. You realise what this means?'

'No, Inspector.'

And cheerful about it.

'It means,' Ghote said, more for the pleasure of spelling it out for himself than for Desai's enlightenment, 'it means that in a period of three months we have had two very elaborate practical jokes played in Bombay. First this donkey business you told me about, and then the shooting of four flamingoes. It is the same hallmark, Sergeant. And it has nothing at all to do with politics.'

Desai took all this in.

'But, Inspector,' he said, 'you told it had to do with politics. We were going to Walker and Walker's to—'

'Hunter and Hunter's, man. And we do not need to go there any more. We need to go to Records.'

'Records? Inspector?'

'To see if there have been any other jokes like this, you fool. To trace the hallmarks of this criminal of ours.'

3

But before Ghote could hurry along to the C.I.D. Records Department to build up on this chance discovery that a monstrous practical joker was at work in Bombay the telephone on his desk pealed out sharply. He picked up the receiver.

'Inspector Ghote here.'

'Ah.'

The man on the other end of the line seemed very pleased to have got hold of him.

'The name's Kamdar,' he said gustily. 'Ram Kamdar. I've been very much wanting to meet you, Inspector, if only over the phone.'

Kamdar, thought Ghote. Where have I heard that name?

'Yes?' he said cautiously.

'Yes. I see this as a position for maximum co-operation. It could be a major departure in correcting a tendency to mutual opposition between our two departments.'

'You are wishing to speak to Inspector Ghote, Inspector Ganesh Ghote?'

'Ganesh,' said the man on the other end of the line in a tone of overwhelming satisfaction.

'I am afraid I do not know who I am speaking to,' Ghote said.

'To Ram, old chap. Ram Kamdar, the Minister's P.R.O.'

That was where he had heard the name. The acting-Director at the zoo had mentioned it. And there had been a circular letter too, he remembered now. He had pushed it away somewhere. And then there had been some gossip when it had arrived: something about the chap being a cousin of the Minister, not

38

the new Minister but the old one, the one who had had to resign. But old Minister or new, he was talking at this moment to the Minister's own personal spokesman.

'Very sorry, sir,' he said hastily. 'There seems to be something wrong with this line.'

That excuse at least was always safe—unless you were speaking to the P.R.O. for the Minister for Posts and Telegraphs.

'Yes. Well, as I was saying,' came the cheerful voice from the Police Ministry, 'I regard this as an open-ended opportunity to set up a new pattern in inter-department relations, Ganesh, old man.'

'Oh, yes, sir. Er—Mr Kamdar.'

'Ram, old boy. Please. Ram.'

'Er—yes.'

'Well, old man, delighted to have established contact. Very important to set up a high level of personal inter-communication, I always say. What?'

Ghote thought it would be safe to make a sound which could be taken for a murmur of agreement, or not. But what on earth did the Minister's P.R.O. exactly want?

The rackety voice started up again.

'Exactly. Exactly. So we must meet. A social occasion would be in order, I think. I regard it as a sub-function of my post to make person-to-person contact with as many people in your department as possible. Though not forgetting the Arts boys, eh? Police Affairs and the Arts,

39

that's the brief. Never forget it.'

'No.'

'It's a question of establishing a general climate of acceptance.'

'Yes.'

'Well, splendid to have heard from you, Gopal—er—Ganesh. And I look forward . . . as I say.'

'Yes.'

'Till we meet then.'

'Good-bye, then,' Ghote ventured.

'Good-bye, old man. Oh. One thing.'

'Yes?'

'The Minister. You will have a result for him soon, won't you, old chap?'

'Soon?'

'Yes. You know how it is at our end. Quick results always help. So make it first thing Monday, eh? Call me at 9 a.m. I'll fix an appointment with the burra sahib. He's in Delhi just now, but his flight gets in early on Monday. Okay?'

'Yes.'

Ghote found it impossible to infuse any enthusiasm whatever into the reply.

The line went dead.

He put the receiver down slowly. This was Friday: that left him only just over forty-eight hours to find the joker. Unpleasant thoughts began emerging like wriggly things from stagnant water.

'Come on, Sergeant,' he said to Desai,

forcing himself into briskness. 'Let's see what we can get out of Records.'

With the sergeant trailing irritatingly a couple of yards behind he made his way rapidly to the Records Department.

And there he found it was indeed a question of 'getting something out' of the department. No one seemed prepared to listen to him. They would talk about anything rather than the dull business of extracting information from the innumberable battered files in their dull green-painted cabinets. They talked about their health and their families, perfunctorily asking after Ghote's first. They talked about sport and about what they had read in the paper. A hathayogi was to walk on water somewhere in the city, a feat that was constantly being attempted somewhere or other, and this seemed to have taken the fancy of everyone Ghote spoke to. Everybody seemed to have taken it into their heads to go and see him, though they were about equally divided over whether he was actuality going to achieve the feat or whether there would be some last-minute hitch. No one would get down to business until they had talked up and down it all at least once. Listening to them with what appearance of polite interest he could manage, Ghote thought about the P.R.O. to the Minister for Police Affairs and the Arts and the deadly last few words of his telephone call.

But at last he got some co-operation. Only to find that practical joking was a classification which the Records Department did not recognise. So depressedly he set himself to whisk through every one of the likely Case Reports for the last six months in an effort to find if any of them were the work of the man who had shot the Minister's flamingoes and kidnapped the Indian Derby favourite.

He was not helped by having Sgt. Desai watch him, as though working one's way laboriously through sheaves of paper was some hitherto unattempted conjuring trick. Luckily the trick was so dull that at last even Desai wandered away. For a quarter of an hour or so Ghote was able to work in concentrated silence. The dust-smelling files went banging back into their cabinets as he finished with them with satisfying frequency. But he came across nothing which looked even remotely like a large-scale practical joke on the lines of the flamingo shooting or the horse-into-donkey trick.

It was at the end of the quarter-hour that quite suddenly he realised that Desai had inveigled most of the Records staff into a game of cards. It was quite blatant. They were squatting in a remote bay between two rows of the tall green-painted cabinets with the cards on the floor. Their voices came quite clearly to him as he worked.

He looked at his watch. It was early for

lunch, but if they were stretching things a bit it was within their meal-break time. He could scarcely object, even though he strongly suspected that the game was actually taking place well inside what should be working hours. He shook his head and drove himself to give full attention to the files in front of him.

But before long the voices of the card-players penetrated again—'Going down for four,' 'Anna in the kitty,' 'Going down for five.' They were playing Rummy, he thought.

And a deep-down whisper of envy crossed the back of his mind. As a boy he had played cards incessantly, and at one time Rummy had been his favourite game. There was a certain amount of skill in it, opportunity for a certain amount of cool judgement. He had been pretty good. That idiot Desai would be hopeless at it.

He pulled himself sharply together and plunged into the dusty files again. But he was aware that the card-game had lasted well into the regular lunch-hour. He decided not to bother to get a meal himself. He had to find out, and as quickly as possible, whether any other large-scale practical jokes had been played in the city recently. Otherwise he was likely to have nothing at all to say when he had to ring that man Ram Kamdar at the Ministry on Monday morning.

It began to get to the very last moment that could possibly be regarded as lunch-hour time and still the game of Rummy went on. It was even apparent that Desai had got himself into debt beyond hope of retrieval. Ghote looked at his watch. He would give them just five minutes more. Until the hour struck, and then he would have a word or two to say.

And with the very next dog-eared file he pulled out all thoughts of the card-players vanished. He was on to something. The case was all in a slim bundle of papers, marked in heavy capitals across the front 'No Further Action.' It concerned an information laid, and later withdrawn, on the part of Sir Rustomjee Currimbhoy, the distinguished Parsi scientist.

As soon as Ghote began reading he recalled the incident. It had happened a full six months before. Sir Rustomjee, who conducted his research in private, had let it be known that he had discovered an extremely cheap means of desalinating sea-water, a project that would make considerable areas of India independent of the treacheries of the monsoon rains. He had summoned the scientific press, who had been excited by the idea. The regular Press had begged to see the wonderful new Indian invention.

And then one of the reporters being shown the test-plant had had the curiosity to peep more closely than was polite and had discovered a small but powerful pump which was in fact taking away the sea-water as it went into the apparatus and replacing it with Bombay's own familiar, muddy-flavoured

44

drinking-water. To make it worse the pump was of English manufacture.

The respected Sir Rustomjee, who had sworn that he had no idea that the pump was there, had become, briefly, a laughing-stock. Clearly here was a case that had such an extraordinary likeness to both the affair of the shot flamingoes and the switching of the Derby favourite that it could hardly but be the work of the same hand. It had all the trademarks: it was extremely elaborate; it must have cost a lot with that special English pump to buy; it hit at a prominent Bombay figure, and it hit cruelly hard. Ghote carefully copied every detail from the file into his notebook.

And when he looked up from this, a quarter of an hour later, it was to find Sgt. Desai at his elbow once more, looking sad but with his eyes filled with wonder.

Under this continued silent scrutiny Ghote resumed his search of the files. But he found nothing more. As he eased apart a crowded cabinet shelf to squeeze back the last bulgy battered file, he decided that he could tell the silent, gawping Desai that the long day had still not been wasted. He had evidence now about three major hoaxes, plainly all from the same hand: with so many opportunities for the hoaxer to have betrayed his identity in some little slip or other he could not believe it would be any longer impossible to lay him by the heels. He must arrange to see his two newly-discovered victims at once.

He turned to Desai.

The sergeant was no longer there. The clock at the far end of the big records room said five past six. Five minutes after the end of Desai's regular working day. Ghote felt oddly cheated.

*   *   *

He had felt increasingly cheated during the rest of that evening. First an impersonal voice at the other end of the telephone at Sir Rustomjee Currimbhoy's house had informed him that Sir Rustomjee did not wish to see any representative of the police about 'the incident in question.' And Sir Rustomjee was the sort of highly respected figure who would have to be dealt with very carefully in face of a rebuff of this sort. Then he had discovered that the racehorse-owner Anil Bedekar, the victim of the favourite-into-donkey trick, generally lived out at his stables not far from Poona and was 'not available' to see anyone until tomorrow. It was only, in fact, by the exercise of considerable persistence that he succeeded in getting an appointment with the great man for next day. He was to meet him in the Members' Enclosure at Mahalaxmi Racecourse before the start of the afternoon's racing. It was the best he could do.

And by the time he had done it the

remaining people he wished to question at the zoo and at the Victoria and Albert Museum had long before left for their homes. He himself had then gone home, where he had spent the remainder of the evening in silent brooding. And, when he did get to see the museum attendants and the junior zoo keepers next morning, it was only to confirm that none of them knew anything.

So it was in a mood of considerable impatience with the meandering chatter of Sgt. Desai that he set off in good time for Mahalaxmi Racecourse. But at least, he reflected to himself bitterly, the man will be some use here. Because he could not disguise from himself as they parked the truck and joined the crowds advancing on the bookmakers' stands that he did not feel at all at ease in a racing atmosphere.

He had never in all his years in the city been up to Mahalaxmi before. The very idea of a race meeting had always seemed appallingly frivolous to him—the people entirely absorbed by a lot of pampered, too well-fed animals, or, if they were women, concerned only with their appearance, and all the money that ought to have been used to buy the necessities of life hopelessly squandered in feckless gambling.

'Inspector, just one moment only.'

Desai gave him no chance to refuse but blundered off instantly towards one of the bookmakers' stands. Ghote stood watching his big, clumsy form in growing exasperation. Then he lost him. He stood and waited, and waited. But there was not a sign of him. And the time for his appointment with this Anil Bedekar was growing nearer.

He turned and marched angrily through the thickening crowds of chattering racegoers, phrases of their eager conversations battering at him from all sides—'Not a horse with red in its name in the first three races, and I always bet on red,' 'But to-day I am trying a treble accumulator,' 'It is all a question of numbers adding up to twelve, you see.' At last he reached the circular Members' Enclosure, pointed out to him by Desai a few moments before he had been sucked into the bookmakers' clutches. And he found the greatest difficulty in getting any farther. He told the tall, turbaned chaprassis on guard at the spick-and-span white-painted gate that he had an appointment with Mr Bedekar, Mr Anil Bedekar. But they remained unimpressed. He told them he was an inspector of police, but even then they seemed to think that preserving the sanctity of the enclosure was more important than any police business. And it was only when he had recourse to a good deal of bluster and shouting on the one hand and dipping his fingers pointedly into his pocket on the other that he got through it all.

In the Members' Enclosure it was at least

48

less crowded than outside. No one here came up to him, as a gaunt, tin-spectacled fellow had done outside, and offered to sell him 'tips for every race, guaranteed tips.' But on the other hand everyone looked so sleek, so contented in the way they were going about their ridiculous affairs that he began to feel himself boiling with a new rage.

Angrily he accosted a white-jacketed bearer and demanded to know where Mr Anil Bedekar was to be found. His unusual arrogance seemed to bring results.

'Bedekar sahib is over there, sahib,' the bearer said, bobbing obsequiously, to Ghote's redoubled annoyance. 'In the shade under the tree there, sahib.'

Ghote strode off in the direction indicated without a word of acknowledgement. How dare the fellow class him with these idle feckless wealthy people.

All round the tree which the bearer had indicated there was a circular white-painted sun-roof protecting an eight-sided white bench with a sloping ornamental back to it. On the bench in quiet conversation were two men. Crossing the unnaturally smooth turf of the lawn towards them, Ghote found little difficulty in deciding which was the racehorse owner.

They were two such very different looking people. The man who must be Mr Anil Bedekar was young, perhaps about thirty-five,

49

and had about him all the signs of wealth and confidence. His cream-coloured suit looked as if it had just come from the hands of the cleaner's, his slightly wavy hair was beautifully barbered, he sat on the white bench with an air of absolute ease. The person beside him— would it be the trainer of the horses?—was a man of fifty of more, a stocky, paunchy individual wearing a shiny dark blue suit of some silky material all creased and bulging. As Ghote approached he saw that as the latter talked he was chewing a paan, vigorously and sloppingly, so that hardly a word he was saying could have been intelligible.

Ghote came to a halt in front of the pair. But the trainer-chap went on talking without even glancing up. Ghote, restraining his impatience, looked with growing displeasure at the wide mouth, through which he occasionally glimpsed the stumps of broken teeth and the rotating ball of the half-masticated paan, and at the pock-marked cheeks and deep-set slit eyes. He wondered how Mr Bedekar could put up with him. But then the racehorse owner must be obsessed with everything to do with the racing business to have been a suitable victim for the joker. No doubt he would tolerate a good deal from someone he believed was training his horses well.

At last there came a pause in the fellow's half-intelligible monologue about various horses and their troubles. 'Mr Bedekar?'

Ghote said.

Neither of the two men on the octagonal bench replied. The older man simply snatched up an expensive-looking pair of racing glasses that hung from his neck and began searching the crowd at the fence round the enclosure, while his employer sat contentedly looking at the immaculate polish of his brown brogues. However after a little the latter did turn and glance up at Ghote.

'Can I help you, my dear fellow?' he said.

'I hope you can, sir,' Ghote said. 'I am a police officer, and I am making some further inquiries about the most unfortunate disappearance of the Indian Derby favourite on the day of the race.'

'Ah, yes.'

'Certain circumstances have recently come to light which make it look possible we shall be able to make more progress in the matter,' Ghote said cautiously.

He saw one lazy eyebrow lift.

'More progress?'

'Yes,' Ghote answered stolidly. 'We hope that by linking the matter with other similar incidents we shall be able to gather enough evidence to discover the perpetrator of the offence.'

'Other incidents? Have the police been unable to prevent the theft of yet more horses?'

Ghote reflected that it was customary for

the very rich to denigrate the police, and at the same time to make sure they paid as few taxes as possible to maintain the force. But he kept calm.

'It is not a question of horse theft,' he explained patiently. 'The other matters concern an unpleasant practical joke that has been played at the zoo in Victoria Gardens, and the recent hoax of which Sir Rustomjee Currimbhoy was victim.'

'Really? How extraordinarily ingenious of the police department to link such unlikely events together in that way.'

In spite of the drawling tone and the extremely British accent Ghote did feel a certain pride in the achievement.

'The three cases bear the marks of the same perpetrator,' he said. 'Someone utterly irresponsible and possessed of a good deal of financial means. And at the same time a person who must have known a great amount about the security arrangements surrounding the horse Roadside Romeo.'

'What's that? What's that? Who's this?'

It was the trainer-fellow. He had suddenly let fall his binoculars, jerked round on the white wooden bench and was now glaring up at Ghote as if he was on the point of smashing him.

'My dear Anil,' the younger man said. 'You should pay attention to other people. This is a policeman. He is re-opening the investigation into the disappearance of your Roadside Romeo.'

A flood of embarrassment swamped through Ghote. How could he have begun his inquiries on such a ridiculous misunderstanding?

Anil Bedekar, squat and ugly in his crumpled blue silk suit, did not seem at all put out.

'New inquiries?' he said. 'I do not want new inquiries or old. If you wanted to make inquiries, you should have made them when the horse had gone. He was safely in my paddocks at Poona when the Derby was due to be run. I could have got him back in time even.'

'In your paddocks?' Ghote asked.

'Do you know nothing?' Anil Bedekar spat out at him.

'My dear fellow,' said the companion, looking blandly up at Ghote, 'you really ought to have aquainted yourself with all the subtleties of that fearful joke, you know. Poor Roadside Romeo was found that evening when the horses out grazing at Poona were brought in to the stables. They say he could have been quietly there most of the day of the Derby.'

Ghote gave him a suspicious look. He had still to recover from the debacle of the start of this conversation.

'My dear chap, I have quite failed to introduce myself. Let me repair the damage.

53

The name is Baindur, known to my friends as Bunny Baindur, and rejoicing in the somewhat splendid title of Rajah of Bhedwar, given to me as an ironic reminder of past glories.'

Ghote could not repress a prickle of anxiety. A member of the smart set. He had hitherto succeeded in avoiding such people. Well, perhaps he could continue to do so. This person, after all, had nothing to do with the matter in hand.

He shifted his stance slightly so that he was directly facing the squat racehorse owner.

'Certain matters have come to light which have enabled us to link the disgraceful business of your horse and other affairs,' he said. 'I am hoping that by learning the fullest details of each case I shall be able to lay the perpetrator by the heels.'

'Go away,' said Anil Bedekar.

But the words were so muttered and so interfered with by the still smackingly chewed paan that Ghote felt he could reasonably ignore them.

'Unfortunately,' he resumed, 'I am not what is called a racing man myself. So a great deal will have to be explained to me.'

Anil Bedekar simply picked up his field glasses again and swept them round the crowd out beyond the neat hedge that cut off the Members' Enclosure.

'Where is that bloody Jack Cooper?' he shot out to no one in particular.

Ghote, unable even to guess whom it was Anil Bedekar was looking for, kept bravely on.

'I had brought a sergeant with me who has a degree of knowledge of all this business,' he said. 'But he appears to have gone off somewhere on his own.'

'Hoi.'

It was a blasted shout from Anil Bedekar. Ghote stopped and looked at him, blinking.

'Mr Cooper. Mr Cooper,' the racehorse owner roared. 'Where the devil have you been?'

Ghote turned to see who this Mr Cooper was. A tubby-looking European, a man well into his fifties with a mop of purest white hair and an extraordinarily suffused red complexion, was advancing towards them over the smooth turf. He wore a pair of white trousers, open by one button at the front, a blue blazer with chirpy metal buttons, a white shirt, which had a large brown stain on the left-hand side and was also open by one button beneath the creased and stringy striped tie.

The Rajah of Bhedwar glanced up at Ghote.

'Poor Anil's trainer,' he said. 'Knows his horses, but a sad trial in many ways, old Jack Cooper.'

Jack Cooper came up to them. He smiled with sharply twinkling eyes. Ghote saw that these were of the very brightest blue. The smile radiated warm cheerfulness.

'Yes, yes,' Jack Cooper said. 'Sorry about

that. Met an old pal. Had to have a noggin, you know. And then he told me this extraordinary story about a chap that can walk on water. He's off to see it happen, too. Fascinating. Had to listen.'

'And what about my bloody horse? In the first bloody race?'

Anil Bedekar's pock-marked face did not show any effects from his trainer's happy friendliness.

'I'll toddle along and see to it, never you worry,' Jack Cooper said to him, giving his white-plumed head a cheerful nod.

Anil Bedekar's mouth set trap-like over his stumpy broken teeth.

'You'd better, Mr Cooper,' he grunted.

'Will do, will do.'

The tubby trainer wandered round in a circle and made his way, weaving slightly, towards a door at the side of the tall, low-roofed building behind them. A thought struck Ghote. He turned towards the Rajah.

'Good lord, yes,' the latter said, in answer to the question Ghote had not yet formulated. 'Drunk as can be. Almost always is.'

Ghote frowned. It was the sort of behaviour he was beginning to expect from anyone connected with horse-racing. His mind came unswervingly back to the subject of Sgt. Desai.

'Yes,' he said to the Rajah. 'As I was telling, I brought this sergeant with me, but he has wandered off. He knows all about this

56

business. But a feckless fellow, as you might expect.'

The Rajah's full, gravely handsome face was lit by a sudden sharp grin, which vanished as quickly as it had come.

'Then perhaps you will permit another feckless fellow to do what he can to enlighten you?' he said.

He stood up briskly. Unwillingly, but inevitably in face of Anil Bedekar's still turned back, Ghote put a question to him.

'Please, do you know the circumstances in which this horse, Roadside Romeo, disappeared?'

'My dear fellow,' he said, 'anyone within fifty miles of poor Anil on Derby Day knew everything, but everything, about the circumstances.'

'Then perhaps if Mr Bedekar is busy . . .' Ghote said.

'My dear old boy, Mr Bedekar is not so much busy as unwilling. He really thought he was going to pull off the Derby this time. And everybody knows that that is his sole ambition in the world. It's a most romantic story. I dare say your sergeant could have told it to you. It's been in all the sports pages time and again. My poor Anil started life as a street boy, you know. He came up here to Mahalaxmi one Derby Day to see what he could beg, borrow, or, I'm sorry to say, steal. And he was so struck with the charming spectacle that he there and then determined he would one day own a racehorse and win the Derby himself. And, by George, this year he nearly did.'

'How was it that this year was especially suitable for him?' Ghote asked.

The Rajah of Bhedwar looked at him with an exaggeratedly surprised air.

'My dear fellow,' he said, 'you have really a very great deal to learn. Do you know, I think there's only one thing for it: we must start at the beginning, and educate you. Nothing else will meet the case.'

Ghote looked at him, trying to conceal the blank suspicion that had swept irresistibly through him.

'That is very kind,' he said, concealing his misgivings hard. 'Could you perhaps tell me first how it is that a horse that is expected to win an important race like the Indian Derby can be stolen from a place like this. I had some difficulty myself in even getting into the Members' Enclosure.'

The Rajah of Bhedwar pulled his beautifully cut cream jacket straight with an air of decision.

'Yes, yes,' he said. 'Details like that can be gone into later. The first thing is to give you as much practical experience of the racing game as we can crowd into one glorious afternoon. Come with me.'

He set off across the neatly clipped green turf and Ghote thought it best to follow, though he was by no means pleased to be leaving Anil Bedekar, grumpily unhelpful though he was.

'As a matter of fact,' the Rajah said carelessly, as he threaded his way ahead of Ghote through the relaxed groups of well-dressed men and bright sari-clad women standing about on the circular lawn, 'poor old Roadside Romeo wasn't pinched from Mahalaxmi at all. He was taken from some stables nearby where our friend Anil had been foolish enough to put him for the night.'

They went out through the gate into the busy, thronged public part of the course.

'Why was this then?' Ghote asked.

'Oh, he thought the animal would be safer where it could be looked after completely by his own syces,' the Rajah said. 'But don't let's bother with these absolutely mundane details just now, old boy. Let's put some money on the first race while the odds are reasonable.'

Ghote smiled a little.

'Of course,' he said. 'Please do not let me disturb your afternoon's entertainment. It is most good of you to answer my questions.'

The Rajah stopped, turned to him and put a friendly hand on his shoulder.

'Not my afternoon's entertainment, old man,' he said. 'Our afternoon's entertainment. You are to be entertained every bit as much as me.'

There was something blandly assuming in

59

the friendliness of his tone which Ghote did not altogether like. But he did his best to smile gratefully.

'I am sure it will be entertaining, as well as instructive, for me to watch you—er—betting and so forth,' he said. The Rajah shook his head, just a little.

'No, old man,' he said. 'Not to watch: to participate. That's the point, you know. You can't learn what racing means unless you've got a proper stake in it.'

He swung round and pointed over the heads of the thick crowd all round them at the row of bookies on their low platforms under the shade of the tiled roof surrounding the bookmakers' ring.

'I rather think I spot what we want just there,' he said. 'From my good friends Shah and Salim. Some really very attractive odds for a certain animal I have in mind. Come on.'

He caught Ghote by the elbow and pushed him along beside him in the direction of a white board hanging from the roof edge bearing the painted names Shah and Salim. Under it was a blackboard on which either Mr Shah or Mr. Salim was busy scrawling ever changing numbers against a hastily written list of horses.

'Yes,' said the Rajah as they got up close, 'not a word to anyone, my friend, but do you see the odds for Cream of the Jest?'

Ghote obediently looked at Mr Shah's

60

notice-board. After some time trying to decipher that gentleman's writing he located a scrawled abbreviation which he took to be Cream of the Jest and saw that the figure '20' was written against it.

'Yes, I see,' he said, not wanting to appear too much of a fool.

'And let me add this,' said the Rajah, putting his hand-some, if a little dissolute, face close to Ghote's ear. 'It's what they call a cert, old man. I have it from the stable.'

Ghote felt extremely unhappy. He realised he was going to have to have a bet on Cream of the Jest. In ordinary circumstances he might not have minded, provided he was not expected to risk too much. After all, the Rajah seemed very knowledgeable about all this business and he had said he had a tip from the stable, which was presumably a good thing. But something not a little worrying had sprung up in his mind: Cream of the Jest was surely the name of the horse Sgt. Desai had recommended. And if anything was certain in the uncertain world of horses and racing, it was that any animal on which Desai put money, unless it was an absolute favourite, was bound not to win.

On the other hand it was not going to be really possible to reject the Rajah's advice.

Inwardly Ghote shrugged. Provided that not too much was involved he would just have to write it off.

He plunged his hand into his pocket and cheerfully pulled out a five rupee note.

'Well,' he exclaimed with a touch of bravado, 'you will have to tell me just what I am to say to Mr Shah, or Mr Salim.'

'Oh, quite simple,' the Rajah replied, scarcely looking at Ghote now. 'You just go up to him and say "A hundred on Cream of the Jest to win" or "Two hundred" or whatever you choose.'

Ghote quickly dipped his hand back into his pocket, scrabbled around and got two five rupee notes between his fingers.

'Yes,' he said. 'Though I think I will be more modest than that. I suppose Mr Shah will consider a mere ten rupees?'

The Rajah turned and looked at him. Ghote found that he was beginning to dislike this habit he had of lazily raising one eyebrow.

'But of course,' the Rajah said. 'He will take any sort of chicken-feed anybody is foolish enough to offer him. And if you want to throw away twenty times a hundred chips, don't let me stop you.'

There was something so utterly calm and ruthless about the way he had said this that Ghote found that the two five-rupee notes between his fingers had slipped back among the rest of his money almost before the words had been finished. He set out in the privacy of his pocket to discover just how much in total he had on him. After a little he decided it must be about fifty rupees.

'Look,' the Rajah said suddenly. 'J. Kumar and Co. is offering 25 to one. Quick.'

Ghote felt his elbow being caught again between four steel-hard fingers and a thumb and before he quite knew it he was standing in front of the white-shirted figure who represented J. Kumar and Co.

'Fifty on Cream of the Jest to win,' he gabbled before the Rajah could speak for him and name a sum he did not even have to hand.

He hauled the money out of his pocket. To his relief it did total fifty rupees. He surrendered it bleakly.

'That's splendid,' the Rajah said. 'Now you will begin to see what it's all about.'

He set off purposely through the crowds again. Ghote followed. He had begun to do various pieces of arithmetic, in each of which the sum of fifty rupees was set against various necessary household purchases.

The Rajah led him to the back of the big grandstand building, white and tall, each of its two end towers surmounted by a just fluttering flag. There were two more chaprassis on duty at the entrance, and one of them stepped in front of Ghote and said respectfully but fiercely, 'Your badge, sir?'

'With me,' the Rajah said carelessly.

The tall chaprassi stepped back.

Ghote followed the Rajah through an ornately decorated refreshment-room and out on to the broad roofed-over terrace facing the white-edged circle of the course. They were near the side of the stand and in a few moments Ghote saw the runners for the first race coming filing on to the course itself through the Members' Enclosure behind them, each with its jockey in bright racing silks on its back and led by a white-clad syce.

The Rajah nudged him and pointed.

'Cream of the Jest,' he said.

Ghote thought the animal did not look as glossily groomed as the others. But he said nothing.

The horses were led down to the tubular structure of the starting gate. A loud buzzer sounded out. The crowd hushed and then jabbered again. There was a good deal of fuss while each animal was manoeuvred into its allotted compartment. Ghote started wondering what proportion of the lost fifty rupees he could successfully conceal from his wife.

The last recalcitrant animal was tugged into its place under the disparaging eye of the dark-suited Starter, long whip in hand. Then this authoritative figure took the microphone from its hook at the side of the gate and made an announcement that the horses were under orders. Ghote, even before the Rajah had explained that he could now in no circumstances get his money back if Cream of the Jest failed to win, felt a sudden totally unexpected tightening-up of excitement.

He found that he was actually considering the possibility that the wretched horse might get past the post first. Fifty rupees at 25 to one, surely that would mean 1,250 rupees. Think of all the problems that—

The starting gate clanged open. There was a concerted rising murmur from all parts of the course 'They're off,' and the six horses in the race strode out over the even turf before them.

Ghote's mouth was very dry.

For a long time the six horses stayed bunched tight together, fighting it out stride for stride, the open patrol car skimming along beside them on the outside of the course, its white-walled tyres dazzling in the sunshine. The Rajah at Ghote's side was commenting on various aspects of the jockeys' riding. Ghote heard not a single word he said. He could think of nothing but the horse Cream of the Jest down there in the bright sun in front of him. Would it suddenly begin to emerge from the nick of bunched animals? Or would another horse? Would Cream of the Jest even begin to fall back, as with that damned Desai's wretched money on it it was almost bound to do?

He craned forward, eyes stinging with the effort of picking out the vivid green shirt with a white band on it and the green and white quartered cap of the jockey, his jockey. And still the whole field remained obstinately bunched together.

And then, as he had all along known would happen, the green and white cap began slipping towards the back of the bunch. Soon the whole horse could be clearly seen there on its own. The jockey was lashing at it frenziedly with his whip, but Ghote knew that this was no more than the frantic actions of someone who knew his case was hopeless. It reminded him vividly of Desai trying to explain himself out of something under the cold gaze of one of the D.S.P.s.

Before long a large and ever growing stretch of turf was between Cream of the Jest and the rest of the horses in the race. Ghote noted with bitterness that every other animal involved seemed to be capable of going at the same speed as the rest. Only the one bearing his fortunes was unable to put up even an average performance.

He turned to the Rajah of Bhedwar, immaculate in cream suit and heavily knotted striped tie, to whom losing a hundred or two rupees was all in the day's work. He longed to find a really cutting remark springing to his lips. But he knew that all that would come out would be an incoherent reproach.

'Good lord, look.'

The Rajah was suddenly gaping at the green circle of turf in front of them with a look of incredulous amusement. Ghote swung round.

In the few seconds he had taken his eyes off the horses the scene had changed utterly.

Where the five front runners had been striding impressively along side by side in a close bunch there was now only a confusion of rearing horses and flailing-armed jockeys. Something had plainly gone utterly wrong.

'The two leaders tangled,' the Rajah said. 'And look at that. Look at your Cream of the Jest.'

Ghote looked.

Cream of the Jest had been far enough behind completely to avoid the wild mêlée the other horses had got into. And its jockey, for all his frantic whip-work a few moments earlier, had at least been calm enough to take advantage of the situation. He had swung well clear of the rails and was now going round the whole bunch of faltering, caught up leaders. It looked as if nothing could possibly stop him winning, and handsomely.

'One thousand two hundred and fifty.' The number of rupees that would soon be in his pocket flashed clearly and ringingly into Ghote's head. He looked down at the brightly sunlit course in front of him. Cream of the Jest was out there well in front, all alone.

He found that he had actually closed his eyes in delicious terror.

4

When Ghote opened his eyes again it was to hear the yammer of excitement from all over the watching crowd as Cream of the Jest at a price of twenty-five to one passed the winning post and its number was hauled jerkily to the top of the tall indicator mast, shortly to be followed by the white plates with their bold black lettering declaring its distance ahead at the finish to be five lengths.

A flood of wild joy assailed him. Sudden wealth. There without any effort at all on his part was the price of—of what? Say, a first-class air conditioner. One moment hopelessly far away, and the next there for the buying.

He turned to the Rajah of Bhedwar by his side. In spite of everything, he had a lot to thank him for. He found he was being looked at with an air of cool amusement. It acted like a sharp cold shower on the rising warmth of his gratitude.

But he felt obliged to say something.

'Thank you. Thank you. It was most kind of you to offer me the tip. Without it I would . . .'

He gave up.

'Perhaps now you can see how this business can grip people,' the Rajah said. 'And I assure you our poor friend Anil Bedekar was a great deal worse affected than you will ever be.'

Ghote came down to earth. He was not here to place money on horses: he was here to investigate an affair in which the new Minister for Police Affairs was directly and urgently concerned.

'It really did mean a great deal to Mr Bedekar to win the Indian Derby?' he said.

'It obsessed him,' the Rajah replied.

'The person who played that trick on him must have been almost equally obsessed,' Ghote said.

The Rajah was silent for an instant.

'An interesting observation, my dear chap,' he said, with that irritating rise of one eyebrow.

'Well,' Ghote said, feeling the need to defend himself, 'the crime cannot have been committed by any common sneakthief. To transport a horse all the way to Poona so quickly must have meant using a horse-box. Hiring that would have cost quite a lot.'

'An excellent point, my dear chap. You know, I begin to fancy this business of reconstructing your criminal out of the sort of actions he has committed. It gives him a feeling of reality.'

Ghote frowned sharply. It was not for the like of the Rajah to interest himself in such matters.

'The criminal is real enough,' he replied. 'He stole Roadside Romeo.'

The Rajah smiled.

'Very well, he is real. And tell me do you think it was he himself who impersonated the policeman who so conveniently took over the guarding of the horse when the chowkidar's house was set on fire.'

'That is the chowkidar guarding the stables?' Ghote asked. 'And was his house actually set on fire?'

'Oh, yes. A good deal of damage done to the whole area, I believe. But no loss of life, as it turned out.'

'I think,' Ghote said, 'I am dealing with a madman.'

The Rajah laid a friendly hand on his shoulder.

'Don't worry so, old chap,' he said. 'After all, you have me with you.'

'You? With me?'

The Rajah turned and began making his way through the crowd of standing, chattering spectators towards the refreshment-room entrance.

'Yes,' he said. 'The more I think of it, the better I like it. I used to read an immense number of thrillers once upon a time. I always hankered after being a detective, I suppose. But of course it would hardly have done for a prince in those days.'

Ghote pushed his way through the spectators till he had caught up with him.

'Please understand,' he said: 'I very much regret, but it will not be possible for you to

70

share in my investigation.'

The Rajah turned his head and gave him a slight smile. They came out into the refreshment-room, which the Rajah quickly crossed. Ghote hurried after him.

It would not be at all proper,' he said. 'A police investigation is a confidential matter.'

'I shall be perfectly discreet, you know.'

The Rajah spoke without really turning his head.

'No,' said Ghote loudly.

Outside the Rajah paused on the steps for a moment.

'Well now,' he said with briskness, 'what next? Is there anybody here you think it'd be worth seeing? I'm afraid poor Anil is hardly going to be helpful. The truth of the matter is that he is still smarting, I think. Unless he wins the Derby next year, I dare say he'll smart for the rest of his life.'

'And will he win next year?' Ghote asked.

'Oh, I shouldn't think so. I don't think he's got anything in his stables now to touch Roadside Romeo, and he's getting on a bit to win a Derby now. And from all I hear there's some other quite promising nags coming up.'

'Then will Mr Bedekar not want this criminal fellow caught?' Ghote said.

The Rajah turned to him.

'And have the whole business gone over again in the papers when you bring your man up for trial? I don't think so. In fact, we're going to have the greatest difficulty with this end of the business. Anil sacked the chowkidar who let himself be tricked, you know. So heaven knows where he is. And his people at the Poona stables won't talk, not if he's told them they're not to. It's more than their jobs are worth. Friend Anil is not exactly a benevolent institution.'

Ghote felt each of these arguments as a hammer stroke coffining his hopes. He made himself look on brighter things.

'We shall see,' he answered. 'Obstructing a police officer in the course of his inquiries is something that no one can be allowed to do. And in any case there is another side to the investigation I have not yet gone into.'

Suddenly he grinned.

'But one thing before I go anywhere else,' he said with cheerfulness. 'Tell me, please, what is the procedure for collecting my winnings?'

'Winnings?'

'Yes. My twenty-five to one bet on Cream of the Jest.' The Rajah's left eyebrow was going up again in that lazy way.

'But my dear fellow, didn't you see the flag?'

'Flag? What flag is this?'

'The objection flag, my dear chap. You can hardly think that Cream of the Jest had really won after that appalling business half-way down the course. There was bound to be an objection.'

Ghote felt the joy positively running out of him, like water out of a basin.

'My fifty rupees,' he said. 'What happens to them?'

'They go to add to J. Kumar and Co.'s immense profits,' said the Rajah. 'That's racing for you, my dear old chap.'

Ghote watched the image of a magnificent air conditioner march out of his mind and images of a series of quarrels and explanations with his Protima replacing it inexorably. He had been absolutely right never to have anything to do with betting on horses: it was sheer irresponsibility. It was treating life as a joke.

'I am going to see Mr Bedekar,' he announced. 'I am going to see him now. I wish to obtain full details of the criminal act that took place on the day of the Indian Derby.'

Without a word of farewell, he marched off from the Rajah and across to the low white gate of the Members' Enclosure. The two tall turbaned chaprassis seemed this time more willing to let him through.

Lucky for them, he reflected stormily. In a cell they would have been and quick about it if they had tried obstructing him.

And only then, striding across the trim lawn towards the neat tree where he had seen Anil Bedekar before and thought he would see him again, did he realise that the enclosure was almost deserted. No wonder he had been let

73

past without trouble. There was no one there whom he was going to upset. Since he had been here last racing had started. No one was going to stay here where they could not get a good view of the course.

And now Anil Bedekar would take a lot of finding.

Depressedly he turned and made his way out of the enclosure. He set about looking for the part of the course where the best-dressed people might be. Here, he supposed, he might spot the bulging-suited Anil Bedekar.

But before he had got very far he spotted instead someone very different, Sgt. Desai.

The sergeant was mooning along away from the crowds, hands in pockets, looking the picture of gloom. The sight of him came as a salutary warning to Ghote. Had he been looking as ridiculous himself?

He walked forwards briskly.

'Well, Sergeant,' he said in a tone of sharp reprimand, 'and where have you been all afternoon?'

Sgt. Desai looked up.

'Inspector,' he said in astonishment. 'It's you—I—Oh, Inspector, I been looking for you everywhere.'

'Not very hard, I imagine,' Ghote replied, still snarly.

'Oh, Inspector, I had such a rotten afternoon,' the sergeant replied, as if Ghote had politely inquired after his well-being. 'You remember that nag I gave you the tip for?'

'Cream of the Jest,' Ghote said.

He found it was a source of some satisfaction to him that Desai too had been a loser in that topsy-turvy business.

'And Inspector I never put an anna on him. I met a boy I know, and he gave me something else and I changed my mind.'

He would turn out to be lucky like that, Ghote thought. He just would. 'You changed your mind?' he said, forcing himself to be charitable. 'Then you are a luckier man than you deserve to be, Sergeant. There was an objection to Cream of the Jest. It did not win. Perhaps your horse did.'

Sgt. Desai shook his head slowly.

'You just never would understand this business, Inspector,' he said. 'Trouble is you are not what I call a born racing man. That objection only lasted two minutes, then the judges threw it right out. Cream of the Jest won all right. I could have got twenty to one on him.'

'Too bad, Sergeant,' Ghote said briskly, a ridiculous wild joy beating suddenly all over the place inside him. 'That should teach you not to bet. Now, wait here and do not move till I come back. There is someone I have got to see.'

And just as quickly as he could he went and saw that someone, the representative of J. Kumar and Co. And though, incomprehensibly, his winnings did not come to the full tally of Rs 1250, they at least were not far off it.

It was while he was stuffing the last of the notes into an inside pocket that the Rajah of Bhedwar strolled up to him again.

'Ah, my dear chap. I see you've been visiting the good J. Kumar. I was looking for you: I thought you might not have grasped the business about that objection being ruled out.'

'Oh, yes. Yes, thank you, I did,' Ghote said, with a certain amount of distance in his voice. 'And thank you for your tip. And for all the information you gave me to-day. Most helpful. Though it is sad it came to nothing.'

He inclined his head a little.

'And so I'll say good-bye,' he added. 'And thank you once more.'

The Rajah's lazy left eyebrow lifted.

'Not good-bye, old boy,' he said reprovingly. 'We're just off to see Sir Rustomjee Currimbhoy. That is if you care to come along.'

5

As the truck came to a halt outside the big house on the fringe of Malabar Hill which the Rajah of Bhedwar indicated as being Sir Rustomjee Currimbhoy's, Ghote told the mercifully miserable and silent Sgt. Desai to stay where he was. He jumped down on to the wide pavement and made some attempt to smarten himself up. After all, this was supposed to be a social call he was paying, with his friend Bunny Baindur, on the Rajah's acquaintance, Sir Rustomjee.

His friend, Bunny Baindur, Rajah of Bhedwar. The whole idea seemed alarmingly false.

But there had seemed to be no alternative. The Rajah had put the matter baldly: after the debacle of the exposure of his lifetime ambition in the pages of the newspapers Sir Rustomjee was not seeing anybody, let alone the police. The only people with access to the house were friends of his brother, Mr Homi Currimbhoy and it so happened that Mr Currimbhoy and the Rajah's late father had been the closest friends for years. It had been blackmail really, though the Rajah had taken polite pains to wrap it up. But that is what it had amounted to: fall in with my fad of playing detectives and I will make things a lot easier for you, or be the touchy policeman and see where you get.

Ghote watched the Rajah press a languid finger on the big button of the round brass bellpush. From inside the house, an old two-storeyed substantial place with heavy wooden balconies shaded by a huge rambling overgrown tree, there came the slow jangling of the bell. But the big front door was opened unexpectedly quickly and the bearer who stood there was smartly uniformed and spry. Such a man cost money.

He smiled at the Rajah as a familiar visitor.

'Mr Homi is in the drawing-room, sahib,' he said. 'Who shall I say is the gentleman with you?'

He inclined his head, pudgy and yellowish in skin-colour—he would be a Goan—in Ghote's direction.

'I am Mr Ganesh Ghote,' Ghote said quickly, emphasising the 'Mr.'

The bearer left them.

'Ganesh,' said the Rajah thoughtfully, and in a low tone. 'And you must call me Bunny.'

He looked at Ghote's slightly reluctant face with amusement.

'Bunny,' he repeated. 'Everybody does.'

'Mr Homi asks you to come in,' the bearer said, returning on soft silent shoes.

The room into which they were shown was large, and old-fashioned. It looked as if nothing in it had been altered for fifty years. The big dark-red, tall-backed arm-chairs stood each in their seemingly appointed place; the brass trays on much carved boxwood legs beside each of them looked as if they were never by the slightest error interchanged; the serried ornaments on the high wooden mantel-shelf, which surely never had seen a fire, each plainly had its appointed place to a hairsbreadth; the heavy, tassel-edged curtains looked as if even the folds into which they fell were unchangeable.

Against this heavy, ordered background the figure of Homi Currimbhoy seemed at once both floatingly transient and yet part of the fixed whole. He was elderly, probably into his seventies for all the straightness of his back and the smoothness of his pale Parsi face above which the hair was spread carefully across a balding skull.

'My dear Bunny,' he said as the Rajah entered. 'This is nice. It's too long since you came to see us, must have been well before the West Indies Test.'

Suddenly he sprang forward, thrust out his right knee firmly, glanced piercingly in front of him and then made a wide sweeping gesture, grasping what Ghote realised after a second or two must be an imaginary cricket bat.

'Garfield Sobers. Marvellous,' he said.

'He was, he was,' the Rajah said.

Homi Currimbhoy backed up sharply to a bumper, took it on the top of the bat, flicked a glance round to the slips and smiled with relief.

'You'll stay to dinner?' he said. 'Rustomjee will be down in a minute. I think he's up in his study, listening to the gramophone or something.'

He stepped quickly aside from a high one well outside the wicket.

'Yes, well, as I was saying,' he went on, 'we

don't see enough of you, Bunny. Don't see enough of you here, don't see enough of you out there.'

He was looking in the direction of a pair of french windows deeply embowered between their thick red curtains as he spoke, and for a moment Ghote peered out at an only moderately well kept garden and wondered why the Rajah of Bhedwar should be expected to be out in it.

In the meanwhile Homi Currimbhoy was giving the Rajah a straight look.

'Now, out with it,' he demanded. 'Do you play any games at all these days? You aren't out on the cricket pitch, I know. But you used to be pretty good at almost everything that was going. What do you do?'

Bunny Baindur smiled.

'Nowadays,' he answered, 'I'm mostly a detective.'

'A detective? What damned silly joke is this? We can't afford a fellow of your abilities going creeping around with a magnifying glass, you know.'

'A magnifying glass,' the Rajah said thoughtfully. 'Now that's something I hadn't thought of.'

Homi Currimbhoy, looking even more like a will-o'-the-wisp than before, squared up to him.

'You're not serious about this, are you?' he said. 'Being a detective. Wasting your time. Why, you might as well be off to try walking on the water like that extraordinary fellow the papers are so full of.'

The Rajah smiled.

'My dear fellow,' he said, 'all this moral tone is making me forget myself: I haven't introduced Ganesh Ghote to you.'

Homi Currimbhoy swung round and offered Ghote his hand. It was very cool to the touch.

'Delighted,' he said, 'Delighted. Any friend of young Bunny's is a friend of mine. Knew his father in the old days. Some wonderful times we had in his state, you know. Marvellous stable, duck on the lakes. Bhedwar's hard to beat. Or was.'

'Ganesh is a detective,' Bunny Baindur said, with the utmost casualness.

But Homi Currimbhoy was hardly disconcerted.

'My dear fellow,' he said. 'You must forgive me. That young scamp let me go on. To tell you the truth, I dare say I'm a bit obsessed with cricket, you know. Cricket and other sports. They seem to have bulked pretty large in my life, and when a damned fine cricketer like Bunny here won't play, I go off the deep end a bit.'

Ghote was saved from making much of a reply to this by the advent of Sir Rustomjee Currimbhoy. He looked at the distinguished scientist with curiosity while Bunny Baindur performed introductions. He was a solider figure than his brother and looked noticeably younger, though the family resemblance in the oval faces with their long straight noses and long ears was marked. But it was in the eyes that the greatest difference lay. Homi Currimbhoy's were vivid, dancing, alive: Sir Rustomjee's were noticeably more deeply set and had about them a concentrated, zealous wintriness which Ghote found at first impressive and then disconcerting.

For a while the conversation settled on inquiries after relatives of Bunny Baindur's whom the Currimbhoy brothers knew, and Ghote, sitting in the middle of one of one of the tall red arm-chairs, was able to watch them both in silence. It gave him time to analyse what it was about Sir Rustomjee that was so vaguely disquieting. And before long he got it: as the old man talked, across those deep-set wintry eyes every now and again there passed a screen, a look of sudden total uninterestedness that ran upsettingly counter to the passion that seemed proper to the man.

The hoax, Ghote reflected. Had it really hit him as hard as this?

His question was soon answered. The list of friends and relations to be inquired after had been run through, Bunny gestured towards Ghote himself.

'I didn't tell you,' he said to Sir Rustomjee. 'My friend Ghote here is a detective. A regular Sherlock Holmes of a fellow, and I am his Watson.'

'It's time you settled down, young fellow,' Sir Rustomjee replied.

The remark began as a light reproof, but half-way through the screen abruptly descended and it ended as a flat statement. But Bunny Baindur did not seem to notice.

'No, you know,' he said happily, 'I don't think a Watson is quite right. To begin with, I couldn't stand quite such a subordinate role, even to my friend Ganesh here. And secondly I seem to remember the great Holmes had some more active allies. Those boys. What were they called?'

'Sherlock Holmes,' Homi Currimbhoy said. 'I was always being egged on to read him as a boy, but I preferred to be out of doors, you know.'

Bunny Baindur turned to Ghote.

'What were they called, those boys?' he said. 'You must know.'

'I am afraid I have never read the volume in question,' Ghote replied, as little stiffly as he could.

'Sir Rustomjee,' Bunny persisted. 'You can surely help me out.'

'Help you out, my dear boy?'

'By telling me who were the street arabs who used to assist Sherlock Holmes.'

'They were called the Baker Street Irregulars,' Sir Rustomjee replied with an effort. 'But why this sudden interest in them?'

'I was telling you. I'm going in for the

detective business. In fact, that's why Ghote and I dropped in. To solve your mystery of the missing, or rather unmissing pump.'

'No.'

The wintry eyes now flashed cold fire.

Sir Rustomjee looked stonily at the Rajah.

'I wish to hear nothing more of that,' he said.

So, Ghote thought, the joke had been as cruel as that. A clammy embarrassment swept over him. How was he to get away now that the Rajah had put him in this position?

He stood up.

And at once Sir Rustomjee turned towards him.

'My dear fellow,' he said, 'please don't feel that you're unwelcome here. What's past is past, but I don't like having things raked up unnecessarily.'

He cast about for some new topic, and produced one with a quickness that did credit to a long habit of politeness.

'Now tell me,' he said, 'how did you happen to run across young Baindur?'

'We met this afternoon only,' Ghote answered, still feeling decidedly uncomfortable. 'Up at the Mahalaxmi Racecourse.'

Sir Rustomjee was keeping the screen from closing over those deep-set eyes. They even seemed to twinkle now.

'Were you there for business or pleasure?' he asked.

And just in time Ghote saved himself from telling the truth.

'I had the pleasure of winning Rupees one thousand,' he said. 'Thanks to a tip from the Rajah.'

'Then you got more out of him than most people do,' Sir Rustomjee said. 'Bunny, you're a young—'

He turned to address the Rajah. But he and Homi Currimbhoy had left the room.

'Hmph,' said Sir Rustomjee. 'I suppose Homi is insisting on showing him his latest trophies of the chase. You know, that man is seventy-two years of age. Five years older than myself. And he's still totally absorbed by frivolous pastimes like hunting and cricket.'

He smiled.

'Our old father used to say he'd grow out of it all eventually when I used to complain about him,' he went on. 'And I did used to complain. I was a very serious young man, you know, and I thought everyone should be as much wrapped up in some serious subject as I was in my research.'

And with that word the screen did come down. Sharply and it seemed finally. Sir Rustomjee sat in his tall-backed chair and said not a word more. And before long Ghote realised that he had let slip the chance of adding to the conversation in any way that might seem at all natural. Soon he felt the silence growing really oppressive, and there was still not the least sign that Sir Rustomjee's trained politeness had conquered his deep inward-turning.

In the garden it was beginning to get a little dark and the big room was already very gloomy with the heavy draping of the red curtains lessening the light from the windows. It was no longer easy to see Sir Rustomjee's face, protected as it was by a wing on the back of his high red-plush covered chair. But Ghote hardly needed to see the face: the sheer immobility of the body told him that the old man was still plunged in stony blackness.

Abruptly Ghote found he could bear it no longer. For a moment he wondered whether he could get up and just creep away, leaving Bunny Baindur and old Homi Currimbhoy discussing sport wherever they were, and go back to the ordinary round he better understood. But then he knew what he must do instead.

He leant forward in his big chair.

'Sir Rustomjee,' he said sharply.

The old man jerked a little more upright.

'Yes, yes, dear fellow?' he said, though it was evident he had little idea whom he was talking to.

'Sir Rustomjee, you have been the victim of a joke that was most extremely cruel. Almost as cruel as murder. But that is not the whole matter. Other people have been victims also.'

He leant forward intently in the gathering

gloom of the big, heavily furnished room. The eyes in the oval face opposite him seemed to be bright.

Sir Rustomjee,' he went on, putting all he could into each word, 'I am the officer charged with investigating these cases. I wish to prevent the occurrence of anything similar in future. Would you show me your laboratory?'

There was a long silence. But Ghote did not feel the need to say anything more now. He could clearly see once more the deep-set eyes opposite him in the recesses of the tall wing-backed chair. And they were not screened.

A big black marble clock standing in the centre of the white overmantle was ticking softly and discreetly, as it had ticked for years.

'Yes, I will,' said Sir Rustomjee.

*   *   *

As they were about to leave the house by a side door Sir Rustomjee stopped and took a large, slightly rusty key off a hook. A cheerful voice hailed them from behind. It was the Rajah of Bhedwar.

'Off to the lab, are you?' he called. 'Hang on, I want to come too, you know. I can hear Homi recalling his game bags any day: but this is my first chance to do some real detective-work.'

Ghote went cold. For a moment he feared that Sir Rustomjee would change his mind about re-opening the old wound. But the old man's long-nosed, sunken-eyed face remained set and he slipped the key into his pocket without making any acknowledgement of the Rajah's remark.

He stood aside at the slightly crumbly white-painted door and ushered Ghote through, and when Bunny Baindur came up hastily he made no objection.

'Allow me to lead the way,' he said.

Ghote and the Rajah followed him in silence through the now dark garden, sweet with the scent of old flowering bushes, to a narrow gate in the high wall at the back. This seemed to have jammed fast and it needed all Ghote's strength allied to Sir Rustomjee's feeble efforts to free it.

'There has not been occasion to open it recently,' the old man said after it had at last been heaved back.

Once more they went in silence across a narrow side-road, dimly lit by a street lamp at the far corner, and along a lane between two big gardens. This led steeply downwards and within a few moments Ghote could smell the strong odour of the sea and hear the sombre slapping of the well on the rocky shore. On they went without a word, descending sharply with every pace they took. The high-walled gardens on either side stopped and the path continued for a little through an open rocky area. Ghote could see the white line of the surf ahead, stretching on either side in the dark. The smell of seaweed and the freshness of the air blotted out everything else.

The line of the surf was broken only by a rectangular area of black, which Ghote realised in a moment was a big asbestos-clad hut. This must be Sir Rustomjee's laboratory.

The old man marched up to the only door and took the rusty key from his pocket. He fitted it fumblingly into a heavy padlock.

'The door has always been secured by a padlock only?' Ghote asked, as Sir Rustomjee fiddled with the lock in the dark.

'Yes, always just like this,' the old man replied. 'There is really very little here worth a thief's attention, you see. The apparatus is mostly pretty heavy. It would need a lorry to get it away, and I used to give some cash to the chowkidar at the house up there from time to time. He would have raised the alarm if anyone had tried to make off with the whole lot.'

'I see,' said Ghote. 'But he would hardly be likely to hear a single fellow who worked quietly on this padlock with a screw-driver?'

'No, hardly likely,' Sir Rustomjee said sadly. 'I dare say the chowkidar sleeps half the night in any case.'

The padlock sprang open with a heavy click. Sir Rustomjee slipped it out of the hasp and pushed the door open. He felt inside it and found a light switch. A dazzling white bar of light cut out across the rocky foreshore.

Blinking, they entered the hut.

Under the harsh glare of a dozen big flat lights ranged in two rows along the ceiling every detail of the laboratory was mercilessly shown up. Heavy machinery, thick black electrical cables, a wide canvas pipe running out of the far end of the building to bring in the supply of sea-water for conversion, a flat wooden table still littered with papers and sheets of calculations. And here and there in the uncompromising light, patches of bright light-orange rust.

Sir Rustomjee wiped at one of them with his bare hand.

'Well,' he said, 'everything is just as it was the morning the pump was discovered.'

Gote looked round.

'There is a good deal of heavy stuff here,' he said. 'Did you have assistance with it?'

'Yes,' said Sir Rustomjee. 'I had two men. Two men who had been with me for twenty-five and thirty-one years respectively. I can give you their names and addresses, of course. I still pay them a certain sum, though they no longer work for me.'

'And other people must have had access here?' Ghote asked.

'Oh yes. A great many. I was always showing friends over my little establishment.'

The deep-sunk eyes were blank.

'And servants?' Ghote asked.

90

'I suppose they did not often come here,' Sir Rustomjee replied. 'You see we have a field telephone rigged up over there. So there was no need for anyone to come with messages. And my assistants used to make tea and so forth.'

He was silent for a moment.

'Often we used to work late into the night,' he said.

'Yes,' Ghote said. 'But I suppose it would be quite easy to tell whether you were here or not?'

Sir Rustomjee looked at him as if he had not understood what was being said.

'I mean whoever inserted the pump into the system would have known the field was clear,' Ghote explained.

'Oh, I see. Yes. Yes. Oh, you could tell quite easily that we were here. To begin with the machinery makes a certain amount of noise. I have had complaints occasionally from the people in the houses up there. And then, you know, these lights are strong, they show through little holes in the asbestos here and there, even though there are no windows.'

'It could not have been easier to obtain access then,' Ghote said.

He looked at Sir Rustomjee. It seemed to him that the old man was making a special effort to stand particularly upright. He ploughed on.

'The pump, Sir Rustomjee. May I see it?'

91

Without a word Sir Rustomjee led him along the building, stooped beside a thick iron pipe and pointed deep under it. Ghote stooped in his turn. It was at once obvious from this uncomfortable angle what it was that Sir Rustomjee was showing him: a small piece of machinery fixed to a heavy board and crudely connected to a joint in Sir Rustomjee's apparatus.

The words 'Made in Britain' could be distinctly seen.

'I assume the presence of this extra piece of machinery is really quite obvious,' Ghote said.

'Oh yes. If you have occasion to stoop just here and peer into the machinery. But no one had. There was no reason why they should have. This is what you might call a standing part of the apparatus. It was basic to every experiment we made. We none of us had looked at it, except perhaps during an occasional inspection, for years.'

'I see. And you would explain all this to your visitors?'

'Yes, I think so. They ask very simple questions, you know. But they liked to see something.'

'And you gave them pretty simple answers too, didn't you?'

It was the Rajah. He had been standing by the door, looking quietly on while Ghote began his questions. But evidently feeling now it was time he staked out a claim for himself he

92

came forward.

Sir Rustomjee looked at him across the twists and turns of his forlorn apparatus.

'I suited my answers to my company, as you should know,' he said in answer to the question.

The Rajah's eyes lit up.

'So, in fact,' he said with a pounce, 'by no means everybody was told enough to know where to put that pump in.'

Sir Rustomjee considered the point. Ghote, standing near him, saw the effort it cost him not to let the protecting screen slip mercifully over his eyes again. At last he gave his reply.

'It's a good point,' he said. 'And it's about, say, ninety-nine per cent true. I suppose I haven't fully explained the workings of the whole apparatus to more than a dozen people in the last ten years, fellow scientists all of them, from Europe or America generally. I could name you the three much respected Indian scientists whom I would have told. But on the other hand there is nothing intrinsically incomprehensible about the basic apparatus. Any good intelligence could have worked out where to put a pump like that to play that ridiculous trick, especially if they already knew something about the set-up.'

The explanation was delivered entirely to the Rajah, who had in his turn begun to squat down and peer about inside the apparatus. Ghote was able to note that the old man seemed completely to have forgotten his own presence. The Rajah's quick appreciation of the points the old scientist raised was equally evident.

It was plainly time to take back the initiative. Only with what?

'Sir Rustomjee,' he blurted out.

The old man turned towards him reluctantly.

'Sir Rustomjee, I—Er—Sir Rustomjee, do you know a man called Cooper, Mr Jack Cooper?'

It was a foolish question. He fought to keep a rising blush under control.

Sir Rustomjee looked a little irritated. But his instilled courtesy triumphed.

'Yes,' he said unexpectedly, 'I think I do know a Mr Jack Cooper. Or rather Homi does, my brother does. He is one of his turf cronies, a trainer, I believe.'

A thought came into Ghote's head, a glimmer of almost unreason.

'Has he been to the house then?' he asked.

'Oh, yes, of course. How else should I have met him? I very seldom go about anywhere these days. My work, you know, keeps me too—'

And the screen abruptly descended.

6

They had got no more out of Sir Rustomjee. Ghote alternately cursed himself for so clumsily pitching the old man back into the heart of his misery after succeeding against expectation in jerking him out of it and congratulated himself morosely on having at least put a stop to the Rajah of Bhedwar's activities as a detective. Because the plain fact had been that the old man was, if anything, more icily determined to get away from the whole subject of the hoax with the Rajah than he was with Ghote. But neither of them had got a word more about the hoax from him, and soon they had made excuses and left.

It was only as they had parted that Ghote had got an awkward shock.

'I suppose you're off to see Jack Cooper now?' the Rajah had said.

'How did—Naturally, I have to interview Mr Cooper. He is connected with both parties.'

'Well, good hunting, old man. But I don't think you'll see Jack to-night. Anil Bedekar had an unexpected winner in the last race to-day, so Homi told me.'

'I am afraid I do not understand racing results.'

'You should: they affect you. That win means old Jack will be out on the tiles celebrating to-night. I doubt if you'll find him.'

And, infuriatingly, the Rajah had been right. Ghote had spent till midnight searching, asking people who might know the trainer, going to places he was reputed to frequent, and all to absolutely no avail.

Sunday morning found him early in his office, pleased by only one thing, that Sgt. Desai was keeping strict office hours and was nowhere in the building. But there was scarcely any pleasure to be got in that: looming over everything and blotting out any chance of optimism was the thought that the Minister's P.R.O. expected him to telephone in a little over twenty-four hours now with a report that would justify an immediate interview with the great man himself. With, in short, a solution to the whole matter.

He sat at his scratched desk with a pile of scrap paper in front of him and wrote down the name Jack Cooper. He wrote it again. But that did not help connect Mr Anil Bedekar's trainer with those dead flamingoes in the zoo. All right, there was a connection between the two other incidents but—

His telephone rang.

He picked it up in a blaze of indignation. That damned switchboard, they might know he did not want to be disturbed, and to ring his phone with something meant for someone—

'Inspector Ghote here,' he said furiously.

'Ganesh, my dear chap. You are hard to get

hold of. Your switchboard swore you weren't there. But I told them: a conscientious officer on a case. Really.'

The Rajah of Bhedwar.

'What do you want?' Ghote said. Or even snarled.

'Just to make sure you don't make any other appointments for eleven o'clock to-day, old man.'

'I do not know what I shall be doing at that hour. But I am afraid I cannot see you. As you told, I am on a case.'

'We're both on the case, old man. That's why you must be free at eleven o'clock. That man is going to try walking on the water at twelve and we mustn't be late. There'll be an enormous crowd. It's taken everyone's fancy. You know Bombay.'

*   *   *

At first when the Rajah had abruptly rung off Ghote had been just plainly furious. It was bad enough having an amateur like that round one's shoulders, but that he should attempt to start dragging one off to the most ridiculous display the city was likely to see for months was worse.

But as the minutes passed the tiny suspicion that the Rajah's words had just implanted in his mind grew and grew. And consequently when at eleven on the dot the phone rang to say that the Rajah was waiting for him downstairs, he did not hesitate to leave. Because there could be no doubt about it: if ever anything was ripe for the activities of the joker it was this much heralded attempt at this hathayoga feat.

'Ah,' said the Rajah, when he saw him, 'I thought it was about time we got some initiative in this case. Glad you see it my way.'

Ghote was strictly honest.

'I had not thought that this might be a time that the joker would strike again,' he said. 'But when you suggested it, I did see that it was likely.'

'My dear Watson,' the Rajah said with that infuriating raised eyebrow.

And he led the way out of the Headquarters building, down the wide steps towards a waiting taxi.

'I only hope you're right,' Ghote said with sternness. 'Otherwise a great many hours of police time are going to be wasted.'

'Oh, not wasted, dear boy.'

The Rajah held open the taxi door himself.

'Not wasted, dear boy. We're going to enjoy this.'

After that Ghote sat in silence for the whole of the short journey.

As they neared the temple outside which the water walk was to take place their progress got slower and slower. Although it was still well before the much advertised time for the event, and although everyone surely knew that in any case it would start very late, crowds of people of all sorts were converging towards the spot. The Rajah was right: the business had caught the Bombayites' fickle fancy in no uncertain way. Their taxi joined a long line of other vehicles, stopping and starting and edging forward with pedestrians and cyclists by the hundred slipping in between them in a highly dangerous way at the least opportunity.

Eventually their driver turned round, an expression of determination on his bearded face under the soft whiteness of his muslin turban.

'This is as near as anybody could get,' he announced.

Ghote and the Rajah got out and joined the pushing throng on foot.

Stirrings of alarm crossed Ghote's mind.

'If what we think is going to happen does happen,' he said, 'will we be near enough to spot anything?'

The Rajah smiled.

'We think it will happen now, do we?' he said.

Ghote glared at him.

'In any case we ought to be quite close,' he answered.

The Rajah smiled.

'Then it's a good thing I bought the two-hundred rupee tickets,' he said.

This silenced Ghote. Two hundred rupees,

he thought. Each ticket that much. It did not disconcert him that the Rajah had evidently been happy to pay not only for himself at this price but had bought a number of tickets, but it did upset him that such prices were being paid at all to watch such a ridiculous spectacle. Two hundred rupees: a man like that newspaper seller over there might be happy to pull in half the sum every month.

Evidently his thoughts were betraying themselves on his face.

'Of course,' the Rajah said, 'I could have tried to get one or two of the really best seats, the five-hundred rupee block. But right beside the tank there everybody's eyes would be on you, you'd lose your freedom of action. We'll see everything from our humble station.'

The press of the crowd had brought them to within a yard of the newspaper seller Ghote had noticed. He forced his hand into his trouser pocket, pulled out a coin and bought a paper. It was hard to do anything with it in the press but he saw sprawled right across the front page a huge photograph of Lal Dass, the would-be water-walker, and a thick black headline with the words 'Excitement Mounts' on it. He crumpled the paper up in a sudden fit of rage.

Ahead of them now he saw the tall stone gates of the temple with in front the wide square of the tank across which the demonstration was to take place. The still surface of its greenish water was glinting like a mirror in the sun. Directly in front of the tall temple gates with their elaborate carvings of gods and scenes from the epics, the whitewash on them shown up in its successive layers by the glare of the sun, stood one section of the crowd. Already densely packed, they would be among the poorer spectators: a long wait in even the heat of April in their situation was going to be no mean feat of endurance.

The better-off spectators had rows of chairs and an odd assortment of benches arranged in a rough square on the near side of the tank and in small enclosures on either side. A number of awnings of different coloured stripes, some running one way some the other, supported on bamboo poles provided a certain amount of shade.

The Rajah pulled a couple of bright pink oblongs of paper from an inside pocket and looked at them.

'Yes,' he said. 'We ought to try and make our way along there to the left. We're at the side, so we ought to see the fun all right.'

Ghote wanted to say that it was not a matter of fun. But he had not time for talking. Making sure that they got to their 200-rupee seats before anything happened was now a full-time job. Everybody else had already been struck by the same panicky thoughts.

He set his face towards the entrance way between two rope barriers that the Rajah had

101

pointed to and set off to forge his way there.

Suddenly a voice called his name, distinctly and very loudly from some little distance away. He turned in the direction of the sound.

It was Sgt. Desai. Never, Ghote thought furiously, had he seen someone look so happy: A look of radiant bliss was sprawled over the wretched man's fate like a rosy sunrise.

'I am taking bets on how far across he gets, Inspector,' he called. 'Already I have fifteen rupees I am holding.'

Ghote turned away and pretended not to have heard. No doubt the idiot was betting that this Lal Dass would get right to the far side: he would be handing back every anna of those fifteen rupees and much more besides before very long.

The rope barrier was near now. Behind it there was less of a crush. People who could afford 200-rupee tickets did not feel it necessary to arrive as early as those hoping somehow to obtain a free view of something.

At the barrier two huge toughs armed with wooden clubs inspected their tickets and let them through. The Rajah threaded his way along the rows of still half-empty benches. Their seats were right at the front with only a low wooden fence separating them from the area round the tank itself. Already other members of the party were there: Homi Currimbhoy in a spotless white suit with a red and yellow striped tie and a wide-brimmed straw hat was sitting in animated conversation with Jack Cooper, boilingly red-faced, sweating, crumple-suited, but with blue eyes still dancing.

Ghote began to feel that this journey was not going to be such a waste of time after all. He would have a few quiet words with Mr Cooper, and find out just how much he knew, or pretended not to know, about Sir Rustomjee's laboratory. And then a sudden mention of the zoo . . .

But this was a hope that was destined to be deferred.

'Now, let me see, my dear chap,' the Rajah said to him. 'Do you know everyone here?'

He looked at his guests.

'Mr Currimbhoy, of course, you met last night. And Mr Cooper I believe you know. But do you know Ram here?'

Ghote indicated cautiously that he did not. It was hardly likely that he would know any of the Rajah's smart friends, and the man who so far had been referred to simply by the common name of Ram looked very much the sort of person he would never have encountered in the ordinary way. He was dressed decidedly in the western style, with a smartly cut cream-coloured silky-looking suit, a white shirt with a razor-stiff collar and a narrow straight tie in broad horizontal bands of colour. Added to this, his face was rendered almost entirely anonymous by a pair of dark glasses in a heavy white frame.

The Rajah smiled with a sudden flash of fine white teeth, and Ghote experienced an equally sudden interior qualm.

'Well you ought to know Ram,' the Rajah said. 'You and he are in the same line of business. Ram was recently appointed P.R.O. to your Minister.'

Ghote looked at the aggressively self-confident white-framed sunglassed figure in front of him.

'You are Mr Ram Kandar?' he asked.

'And you're Ganesh Ghote,' Ram Kamdar replied. 'Bunny told me he'd bring you along by hook or by crook, and I see he got you.'

Ghote felt a fierce flush of shame.

'I am not neglecting the case of the dead flamingoes,' he said in a flurry of excuse. 'Indeed, I am actively at work as of this present moment. I have reason to believe a similar practical joke is about to be attempted on this present occasion.'

'Yes, Bunny told me about that idea of his,' Ram Kamdar replied. 'That's why I came along too. My duty, you might say. And a P.R.O. is never off-duty, old man. Never.'

He jerked his head forward in what Ghote took to be, with the white-framed sunglasses intervening, a look of shrewd keenness.

Ghote manfully swallowed the bitter pill of realisation that life is always unfair. He faced Ram Kamdar.

'I will not say the matter is totally concluded,' he admitted. 'But I have made a certain amount of progress. I have widened the field of inquiry.'

'Yes,' Ram Kamdar said, cheerfully taking command of the conversation. 'Bunny and I were running over the situation last night, trying to establish a few guide-lines, you know. And we certainly came to the conclusion that what had to be done was to correct any tendency to minimisation. It's obviously a major operation you're up against.'

'Yes,' Ghote said cautiously.

The unexpected confrontation did not seem to be as unpleasant as he had expected. But you could never tell.

Ram Kamdar rubbed his hands together briskly.

'Yes,' he said, 'I think it's a fair bet the whole business is becoming distinctly religion-orientated. Look at the chappie now.'

He turned the two white-framed oblongs of his sunglasses in the direction of the far side of the glassy smooth tank in front of them. Ghote, relieved, looked in the same direction.

Sitting there cross-legged on a small raised platform spread with a roughly-patterned piece of cotton material was Lal Dass. It was easy to recognise him from his numerous photographs in the papers, a somewhat plump man of about fifty, entirely naked except for a clean white loincloth and the thin black sacred thread across one shoulder and his chest. He was gazing placidly at the scene in front of him, apparently oblivious of the crowds, the nearby busily conferring European television team, the shouts of the hawkers of cool drinks, newspapers, garlands and kum-kum powder and the general hullabaloo as those who considered themselves latecomers fought to get to their places.

Ghote craned forward to look at the hathayogi. Not so much because he was particularly interested in the figure at the centre of what he had always known would be a noisy and elaborate fiasco, but because he was extremely anxious not to get involved in any further conversation with Ram Kandar, that living representative of the Minister. He abandoned now all ideas of dealing with Jack Cooper: discussing any aspects of the case in front of a man who might report his every word direct to the top was unthinkable.

So he peered and peered at the plump cross-legged figure on the far side of the tank. One thing looked plain enough: the fellow was hardly the person responsible for all the publicity. He was much too quiet for that. No doubt he had been got hold of by some sharp operators who intended to make a good thing out of what was no doubt a perfectly genuine attempt to perform a really extraordinary feat.

Ghote looked at the tank. It stretched for about fifteen yards between him and the hathayogi and was perhaps three yards wide, a green-black, still, unbroken stretch of water. Could anyone ever possibly simply get up and walk across it, as if it was glass? Some strange things certainly did happen sometimes.

Time passed. The others were talking among themselves, and all the seats around them had now filled up with excited people. It was like some sort of monster party, with old friends and acquaintances greeting each other across the intervening heads and a great deal of laughter and pleasantries. But Ghote succeeded in relegating it all to a distant chatter. The Rajah, luckily, was too absorbed in being greeted by people he knew, who all seemed anxious to remind him of their existence, to do any more about playing at being a detective and he was mercifully left alone.

Over the other side of the tank the hathayogi seemed to be in a rather similar situation. There too there was a great deal of excitement, with people running up with messages and conferring and having heated exchanges of various sorts and at the still centre of it all one person who seemed quite oblivious of what was going on. Even when dignitaries from the centre, most expensive seats were led up to him he seemed scarcely to notice their existence, giving only occasionally a mild quiet inward-looking smile. And he betrayed no more interest when they were led away again to examine the tank itself, poking at the surface of the water with great earnestness and much public-display nodding of heads.

And then, well after the advertised time of the event, things at last began to happen.

The various dignitaries began returning to their seats from their inspection of the tank— one had even plunged his umbrella deep down into it and part of his forearm, regardless of any possible damage to either. From the crowd, which now stretched so far into the distance that those at its edge could not possibly see anything of the proceedings, there came a concerted shift forwards and a low unison murmur. Lal Dass, smiling serenely and taking no notice of the deferentially whispering men on either side of him, stood up. For half a minute perhaps he remained upright looking placidly at the water of the tank as it in its turn regained the placidity it had possessed before the experimenters had got at it.

A complete hush fell on the crowd, from the elect in the 500-rupee seats to the poorest of the poor seeing nothing at all in the distance. Slowly Lal Dass began to walk down the steps towards the water.

Ghote found he could not take his eyes off him. He knew at the back of his mind that he ought to be darting discreet glances all round at a peak of alertness for any signs of possible sabotage. But the gentle serenity of the yogi held him transfixed. He felt through and through that he was going to see a quite extraordinary feat. He was going to see a man, a heavy-looking man, solid and well-fleshed, walk airily over the still surface of the tank in front of him.

Lal Dass reached the side of the tank. Again he stood for a long half-minute, looking, not so much at the mirror flat surface, as into some far, far distance of the mind.

And at last the moment came. Calmly, wonderfully confident, Lal Dass stepped boldly forward.

And toppled straight under the thick green water.

7

The same silence that had held the huge crowd watching Lal Dass suspended in one single hush as the hathayogi had taken his stand at the edge of the tank in front of the big temple continued for a few awe-struck instants after his disappearance under the greeny-black water. And then like a gathering whirlwind a single enormous communal squeak of indignation wound its way up from every side, from every outraged throat.

And Ghote realised that the joker had

played his biggest joke of them all. He had expected that in some way Lal Dass was to be hoaxed: instead all that huge crowd, from the ones that had paid five hundred rupees for the privilege to those that had endured for two or three long hours the heat of the sun, had been the joker's victims.

And now they were all voicing their feelings, explaining them away nineteen to the dozen, pointing out to each other in a wild clamour of jabbering how utterly everybody else had been tricked by the whole fantastic business, gesturing, shouting, cursing. Ghote remained silent, thinking.

And all at once he realised the most astonishing fact of all: Lal Dass was still there, still under the water. He had taken that step, toppled incongruously forward into the green-black water, but then he had not splashed upwards walrus-like to the surface. He was still under. It was just possible to make out in the murky depths the vague white area of his muslin loincloth.

Ghote jumped to his feet and scrambled over the low wooden barrier in front of him. No one seemed to be paying the least attention to the yogi. Even his attendants were busy explaining away to each other with the rest of the huge concourse. Nobody had eyes for the tank at all.

Ghote ran round its stone-edged sides till he reached the place were Lal Dass had stepped in. He crouched quickly at the edge of the water and peered downwards.

Yes, the yogi was there. Tranquil and unmoving, in a gently curled-up position, the faint ripples of his fall into the water still stirring very lightly the floating ends of his loincloth.

Ghote took a quick breath and dived head-first in beside him.

The water was deliciously cool and from underneath seemed wonderfully green instead of black and murky. Peering through its translucent depths as his feet found a slimy bottom he located Lal Dass. The heavy yogi's forehead was just touching the green-over stone slabs of the tank's bottom, and the rest of his body appeared to be floating above the head. Ghote put his arms under the naked smooth flesh in a scooping gesture and levered himself upwards from the bottom.

To infinite relief the yogi moved. He had feared somehow that the body would mysteriously resist all his efforts. But slowly and heavily it came to the surface and Ghote came with it. He found he could just touch the slime of the tank bottom with the toes of his shoes and still have the top of his face out of the water with his head thrown back.

'Help!' he called. 'Help, somebody, help.'

He had to call several more times, but at last Lal Dass's attendants realised his predicament. Some of them came to the tank

edge and shouted instructions, which Ghote
was unable to hear as his ears were just below
the surface of the murky water. Others turned
to tell people around what was happening.
Eventually two of them knelt at the side of the
tank and with tentative pawing gestures urged
the big smooth body of their master towards
them.

Ghote, his feet slipping and sliding, pushed.
And in the end he got near enough to the edge
to get a shoulder under the inanimate form of
the yogi and heave. Now a few more people
joined in, catching hold of an arm or a foot
and puffing, some in one direction, some in
another. Between them all they got Lal Dass
laid out beside the tank, a big mound of
golden flesh, smooth and unresistant.

It was Ghote, dripping and clammy, who
after he had struggled out of the tank himself,
put his ear to the yogi's chest and pronounced
that the heart was beating.

'My dear chap,' a voice said in his ear, 'you
really oughtn't to be plunging into the water
and so on, you know.'

His clothes clinging, wet and stiff, to his
body, he swung round to face the Rajah of
Bhedwar.

'He would have drowned,' he said crossly.

'Oh, not really, old man. And in the
meantime, you know, we've work to do. Now
we've got the initiative, we mustn't let it go.'

Ghote felt no better for realising that this

had a large element of truth in it. Someone had succeeded somehow in convincing Lal Dass that he was going to be able to walk on water. That was plain. And at the moment of his discomfiture the hathayogi was most likely to give them some idea of who it was. Only . . .

He looked down at Lal Dass. His heart might be beating, but it was plain that it would be some while before he was doing any talking.

'It's quite plain to me what must have happened,' Bunny Baindur said.

Ghote realised miserably that it was far from clear to him. He took the top of his jacket between a finger and thumb of each hand and tried to lift it clear of his back so that it would begin to dry off.

'Yes,' the Rajah said. 'I dare say you read in the paper: the poor old fellow had already taken a few steps on water, here on this tank in the early hours of one morning. So someone must have done something to the water to make it possible.'

Ghote wrenched his mind away from the clamminess round his waist, which he could think of no way of dealing with in public. He concentrated on the problem the Rajah had propounded. An idea came to him.

'Perhaps if a heavy sheet of glass had been put just below the surface?' he said.

And immediately he was overwhelmed with a sense of how ridiculous the suggestion had been.

'But no. No,' he stammered. 'It would not be possible. It must be some other way. Air. Perhaps it was with air. Somehow.'

'No,' the Rajah said thoughtfully. 'I have a feeling you're on to something, old boy. A big sheet of glass, plate glass, just below the surface. It would do it, you know. Come on.'

He swung round and started off through the thinning crowd at a great rate. Ghote followed him, without having any clear notion what he was doing.

'It's just possible the glass will still be somewhere about,' the Rajah said. 'Our chap might be trying to get rid of it at this moment.'

Ghote broke into a jog-trot. He found with satisfaction that it caused his clothes to billow out away from his body. But it was with much less satisfaction that he registered that once again the Rajah was being the detective while he himself simply tagged along behind.

They made for the back part of the temple where there was a huddle of huts where the vendors at the various stalls round the building lived.

They found the glass with ridiculous ease. It was propped in a small rubbish-filled alcove just at the back of the temple, and it was very plain what it had been used for. The green slime from the tank still adhered to its surface.

But there was no one in sight who looked as if they had the remotest connection with their discovery. Even the Rajah was a little at a loss to know where to go from there.

'We'd better put a couple of men to watch it,' he said, looking at the long sheet of glass with one of its ends cutting into the accumulation of rubbish in the alcove and the patches of slime on its surface turning from green to a dried yellow.

'It does not look as if the joker intends to come to collect it,' Ghote replied. 'And in any case, when people realise it has been left only, someone will take it to try to sell.'

He found himself determined not to allocate men of the Bombay police to any duties at the mere whim of this Rajah.

The Rajah stood for a few moments looking thoughtfully at the glass.

'You know,' he said at last, 'I think some lunch.'

'Yes, yes,' Ghote agreed quickly. 'You go and get some lunch. I will arrange to have someone keep a watch on Lal Dass. That is where we want a man. As soon as he is fit to speak, I must have a private talk with him, away from all those hangers-on.'

His decisiveness paid dividends. The Rajah at once looked positively wistful.

'You will keep in touch, old man?' he said. 'Where can I get hold of you?'

'There is always my office,' Ghote said, feeling for the first time since he had met the Rajah a certain magnanimity.

'Yes, yes, your office. Of course.'

115

They went their separate ways.

*   *   *

At his familiar, scratched desk in his office, with the grease spotted newspaper wrapping of a hurried lunch just tossed into the wastepaper basket, Ghote began drawing up a list of the questions he would ask Lal Dass. On the way back from the temple he had had an opportunity to think about the whole business of the joker without interruption and he felt now he knew what he wanted to ask.

The yogi had been still deeply unconscious when he had left, but he had spotted Sgt. Desai mooning about, doubtless avoiding the people he had taken bets from, and he had very firmly ordered him to stay with Lal Dass and report by telephone the moment he showed signs of returning to consciousness.

He pursed his lips in thought.

There was still very little time before he was due to ring Ram Kamdar and arrange to see the Minister on his return from Delhi. But all the same he thought—

The telephone rang. He snatched it up. '

'Desai? He is coming round?'—

'Inspector Ghote?'

It was the clerk in the hall downstairs.

'Yes? What is it now?'

'Mr Ram Kamdar to see you, Inspector.'

'Very well, very well. Have him sent up.'

He was not exactly delighted. But on the other hand he was not as appalled as he would have been a few hours ago.

A peon knocked on his door and ushered Ram Kamdar in. He strode across the little office, his hand thrust forward.

Ghote hastily pushed back his chair and held out his own hand.

'Ganesh, old man. I had to come down to Headquarters here, and I thought I'd drop in. I missed you after that religio-social disaster this morning, and I wanted to hear your insights on the whole concept.'

Ghote wondered how to reply. Happily the telephone shrilled again.

'Ah,' he said into it. 'It is Desai now?'

'Bunny Baindur actually, old man.'

The voice rang out loudly and confidently. He realised that he had not got over his aversion to it as much as he had thought. He held the receiver a little away from his ear.

'Yes?' he said with extreme caution.

'I have news for you, old man.'

'News?'

'Yes, I've cracked you case for you, old boy. Wide-open, as they say.'

Ghote clapped the receiver back against his ear. He shot bolt upright in his chair.

'Well, listen,' he said. 'I have news for you too. You ringing up like this has just confirmed what I had begun to suspect this morning. This funny game of yours is up. Definitely. Where are you at this moment?'

He barked the question out. There was a long pause at the other end of the line. Ghote listened hard to the continuous heavy crackling. Then the Rajah's voice, the joker's voice, came again, rather quietly and thoughtfully now.

'I'm up at my shack at Juhu. Ran up here to get a bite of lunch, actually.'

'Very well,' Ghote said. 'I am coming to see you. Do not leave.'

He slammed down the receiver and looked up at the big, glossy-looking form of Ram Kamdar.

'Mr Kamdar,' he said, 'I regret, but I have just had a phone call that demands immediate attention. I must leave now.'

'But of course, old man,' Ram Kamdar said. 'In the context of a job like yours these sudden meaningful decisions obviously have to be taken.'

He looked abruptly pleased with himself at this success in fitting in a small awkward lump of material into the smooth shape of his existence.

He stood aside as Ghote picked up his notebook, fitted it into his pocket and gave a final glance round to make sure he had forgotten nothing. Then, as Ghote went ahead of him out of the little room, he laid a friendly hand on his elbow.

'Just one thing, old man,' he said.

'Yes?' Ghote answered, his mind busy looking ahead to his forthcoming encoutner.

'My boss man, you won't forget he'll be back from the Centre tomorrow morning? You'll be able to show him some sort of end-product?'

Well, Ghote thought, I certainly will.

But he hugged the notion carefully to himself.

'I will arrange an appointment per telephone,' he said.

*   *   *

It took him a full half an hour to get to the Rajah's shack out at Juhu Beach, his truck creeping cautiously for the last mile along a sandy lane between high hedges and then stopping at the edge of the huge sweep of buff-coloured sand beside a clump of three tall feather-headed palms. Ghote got out and walked the hundred yards or so across the shifting, slippery sand to the shack, a substantial new bungalow with a low, cool overhanging roof.

He knocked at the front door. It was opened by the most sombre-looking Sikh he had ever seen, an immensely broad-shouldered man with a fierce bar of black matted eyebrow above each dark, deep-set eye and a busy crescent of beard all round the lower half of his face. At his side there hung a kirpan, traditional knife of the Sikhs. But this one had a sternly practical, everyday-use look about it that was far removed from any notion of tradition.

Ghote gave him his name and asked for the Rajah of Bhedwar.

'Wait,' said the Sikh, and only afterwards added a muttered, 'Please, sahib.'

The door was shut swiftly and blankly in his face. He stood looking at a scatter of marigolds, the only flowers in the sandy square surrounded by a straggling hedge of kika thorn, that represented the shack's garden.

Eventually the door opened as swiftly as it had been closed.

'Come this way. Please.'

Ghote followed the man into the house. They went through a broad entrance corridor and then the Sikh threw open a heavy teak-wood door and ushered Ghote forward. The room he found himself in was newly but heavily furnished, mostly in oiled teak. There were a number of cane-backed arm-chairs, a low teak table with an array of bottles on it under one of the windows, a big gold-coloured air-conditioner humming away in one corner, and, slap in the centre of the room a heavy card table at which sat the Rajah of Bhedwar, a complicated game of patience laid out in front of him.

He looked up as the grim black Sikh made him a deep salaam and announced Ghote in the manner of someone punctiliously carrying out a loathsome duty.

'Ah, there you are, old boy,' he said, not moving from the array of playing-cards in front of him. 'Now what's all this you were telling me?'

Ghote confronted him sternly.

'I was telling that it is you yourself who has committed these jokes,' he said. 'Who else both knew Mr Bedekar and Sir Rustomjee, and was a good shot also. I think you did your best, too, to put Mr Jack Cooper in front of me, but I happened to hear Mr Currimbhoy praising your shooting when we called on him. And then when you led me so easily to the plate glass used to trick that poor Lal Dass, it was altogether too much of a coincidence.'

A look of rueful frankness spread across the Rajah's fully handsome face.

'Well,' he said, 'you've been too smart for me, old man. I have to hand it to you.'

But Ghote was in no mood to be disarmed.

'Your conduct has been utterly irresponsible,' he said. 'Not only have you put the Police Department to a great deal of trouble to end your activities, but you have caused the loss of a large sum in public funds.'

'Yes,' said the Rajah. 'Very wicked.'

He slid one long line of playing-cards up into a neat pile and tapped it.

'I have yet to consider the exact form the charges will take,' Ghote said implacably. 'But you can be certain I will see that no item is omitted.'

The Rajah leant back in his chair.

'But, you know,' he said, 'there won't actually be any charges.'

'What do you mean?' Ghote snapped. 'You need not think this is something you can bribe or bully your way out of.'

'My dear fellow, I'm not in anything. There's no need to resort to bribery.'

'What do you mean 'not in?''

'Just that, old man. Not in any trouble that needs getting out of. You'll see what I mean when you come to frame those charges of yours. They won't stick.'

Ghote glared at him.

'Just think, old boy. Poor Anil Bedekar's Derby favourite, do you really think I employed anyone to take that away who would for one moment admit I had anything to do with it?'

A spasm of fury flamed in Ghote's eyes.

'We shall see about admitting,' he said. 'Wait till we get them to police headquarters.'

The Rajah smiled with a flash of too even white teeth.

'First find them, old boy. And I'll even give you a clue. You want to go off to Bhedwar to look. They all come from there. And somehow, you know, in spite of being just a distant corner of the great state of Maharastra, Bhedwar is still remarkably loyal to its deposed Rajah.'

For all his anger Ghote saw the force of what the Rajah had said. Finding who had helped substitute that donkey for the Derby favourite when no one in Bhedwar would be prepared to talk was hardly a feasible proposition.

'All right,' he said, 'but the man who shot those flamingoes was not helped by over-loyal retainers.'

'No,' said the Rajah. 'He wasn't. He wasn't helped by a solitary soul. He actually used a game rifle bought anonymously specially for the occasion and now somewhere under the sea. And he didn't leave a single other clue, did he?'

For all the open insolence of the query Ghote had to admit that the only answer was that the killer of the flamingoes had not left any clues. His only hope had been to link the bullet recovered from the last of the dead birds and the cartridge he had found in the clock tower with the gun that fired them, and that had just been effectively squashed.

He ploughed on, but hardly with any hope.

'But I think it was you yourself who put that pump in Sir Rustomjee's apparatus,' he said. 'That is breaking and entering, a serious matter.'

'Most serious,' the Rajah agreed. 'And you'll find my fingerprints in the laboratory too.'

Ghote could not stop the gleam of hope springing back.

123

'But of course,' the Rajah said, drinking this in, 'I have every right to have my fingerprints here and there on that apparatus: Sir Rustomjee showed it to both of us. Remember?'

It was the final blow. The traces of that crime had actually then been wiped out under his own eyes.

'I suppose the man or men who deceived Lal Dass came from Bhedwar also?' he asked miserably.

'Very probably, very probably.'

Ghote looked at the Rajah almost desperately. He was flipping together the remaining long lines of cards from his patience game with all the dexterity of one who was well used to handling the slippery rectangles of pasteboard. It was a dexterity which long ago Ghote had prided himself on possessing too, and even amid his present preoccupations he felt an odd pang of envy for someone who could still afford to devote time to the beguiling wastefulness of playing cards.

So when he came to address his next remark to the Rajah his voice had lost something of the angular severity it had possessed up till now.

'I must admit you appear to have pulled it off,' he said.

The Rajah's eyes flickered up to his face for an instant, a twinkle in them still.

'But perhaps,' Ghote went on, in his

mellower mood, 'I can satisfy myself without initiating a prosecution. All that will be necessary would be to obtain your absolute assurance that nothing similar will ever happen again.'

The cards were now in two neat packs side by side, a red-backed one and a blue. The Rajah raised his eyes from them.

'But, my dear fellow, I've just developed a taste for it all. It wasn't intended exactly to be a career when I began. I just got that idea about poor Anil and did it. But one thing led to another, and now I'm quite hooked.'

He regarded Ghote blandly.

Ghote's mellowness began to harden.

'And do you know?' the Rajah went on in the same cumulatively irritating drawl. 'Do you know that Minister of yours doesn't seem to have learnt his lesson. I mean, he ought to have taken the hint when I popped off the first of his wretched flamingoes. But to set the police on to me, and such a damned astute policeman too as it turned out. Not exactly repentant.'

Ghote thought he saw what was coming next. He made attempts to deal with it.

'As I told,' he said, 'in spite of the great sums of public money that have been wasted thanks to your irresponsibility, I think there would be no need for official action, provided that all such activitites cease as from today's date.'

The Rajah did not at first reply. He took instead the red-backed pack of cards and shuffled them with a sudden quick flick of lithe wrists. And again Ghote could not keep his rogue eyes off the little act. He could not help noticing the extreme dexterity with which it was done. It looked as if the cards had been slipped into each other in neatly alternating slivers of two and three with an astonishing regularity. He himself had not always managed as much even in his youthful heyday. And of course now . . . his fingers itched.

And he found that the Rajah's limpid brown eyes under the fine arch of the brows were looking up at him with a new note of interest.

'Why, my dear old boy, I do believe you're a card-player.'

'No.'

The denial shot out with ridiculous force. Ghote felt it at once. He struggled to make amends.

'That is to say, of course I have played cards—as a boy. But I regret I consider it a totally boyish pastime. Yes, most definitely a shocking waste of time.'

'A shocking waste of time, eh?'

The Rajah looked at him with amused speculation.

'All right, my dear Inspector. I'll tell you what. I'll play you at cards.'

'I regret—'

'No, wait a minute.'

126

The Rajah's raised hand was gently admonitory.

'Wait till you've heard the whole deal, old boy. I'll play you at cards for what you want: an assurance that practical joking ceases as from to-day's date. There you are. How about that?'

Ghote sat in silence. He could not frame a reply. He tried to persuade himself that this was because he was staggered by the effrontery of the Rajah's proposal. But he knew that this was only partly true: he also desperately wanted to agree to it.

'I regret,' he brought out at last, 'that such an idea could not be acceptable to a police officer.'

He found he was standing in an extremely rigid attitude in front of the card-table, and tried unsuccessfully to force himself into a position of relaxed authority.

'But why not, my dear chap? Look, what have you got to lose? Well, if you do lose some paltry sum of money, you can take it out of expenses. Put it down to payments to an informer. That would be rather nice. And if you win, you've achieved your object. And I assure you, there's no other way of doing that.'

The Rajah took the blue-backed pack and shuffled it with the same skill he had shown before. Ghote, unable to take his eyes off the flittering cards, felt his mouth actually water.

'Well,' said the Rajah, 'is it a bet?'

'How much cash do you expect me to

stake?' Ghote asked.

It was weakness. He knew it.

The Rajah smiled. How intolerably regular those white, white teeth were.

'Oh, I'll let you off lightly, old boy. The Police Department is terribly poor. Or so at least that appalling bore Ram Kamdar keeps telling me.'

The limpid almond eyes looked into Ghote's for a moment, calculating.

'Shall we say a thousand rupees?'

Ghote, who had known with cold certainty from the first that there was no question of using Police Department funds for as irresponsible an idea as this, felt his heart give a single pound of delight at the mention of the sum. It was just under the amount he had won on Cream of the Jest. There would be a complete appropriateness about risking it in this cause.

'Yes, I will play,' he said.

The Rajah's long-fingered right hand swept down like a claw on the red-backed pack.

'Gin Rummy, I think,' he said.

'All right,' said Ghote.

The Rajah looked up and gave him a wide smile.

'Now we shall see some fun,' he said.

8

The Rajah of Bhedwar pushed aside the red-back pack of cards and took up the blue.

'Pull up a chair, old chap,' he said to Ghote, 'and we'll begin.'

Ghote looked round the cool white-walled room and spotted a heavy teak dining armchair. He slid it over the smooth wooden floor, set it at the green-baize table opposite the Rajah and sat down. Without a word the Rajah cut for dealer. Ghote in his turn cut too. The Rajah won. Expert as ever, he dealt the ten cards each.

At the very sight of his hand, all Ghote's playing instincts revived buzzingly in his head. He summed up his position in a fever of delighted speculation. He had fair cards, no more. Quickly he calculated the chances of improving them.

Opposite him the Rajah drew his first new card. Without any change of expression he put down his hand. Ghote looked at the array of cards. They all melded neatly together, a gin—and with hardly any play involved.

With a sudden sweep of depression Ghote laid down his own cards. They could not have served him worse.

'Hard luck, old chap,' the Rajah said.

He reached across to the teak side-table

129

with the bottles on it, flipped open a drawer, pulled out a scratch-pad and noted the score.

Ghote gathered the cards together and shuffled. The sudden sweat that had sprung up on his palms at the quick advantage the Rajah had gained made the cards sticky to his touch. He shuffled them in clumsy lumps which infuriated him.

And the second deal proved no more happy for him than the first. He held out a little longer but before long the Rajah was calmly adding a moderately hefty total to his original score. Ghote leaned forward and looked at the pad.

On the next round the Rajah could hit a hundred, even with moderate luck. He bit at the inside of his lower lip.

But as he picked up the new hand the Rajah had dealt him his spirits soared. Rapidly he sorted the cards round. Really, this was as promising a lot as he could have wished for.

They drew a card each in turn. Ghote surveyed his hand. This last draw was ideal. He decided to take a risk. He would go down at once, on his present fairly high total, and count on the Rajah being caught off balance.

He flipped the cards down on to the green baize.

The Rajah studied them for a moment without putting his own hand down. And then one by one he laid his cards on the table. Each single one but the last melded into Ghote's hand. There was no need to tot up the score. The Rajah had won the game with points and points to spare.

Ghote looked at the array of cards upside down in front of him, three jowly kings, four sixes laid neatly black and red black and red, a sequence of spades. He thought: So now I have almost given official permission to this man to play whatever practical jokes he likes on the Minister for Police Affairs and the Arts.

'You had some lousy cards, old chap,' the Rajah said.

'And I lost,' Ghote snapped back.

The Rajah swirled the cards together.

'Tell you what,' he said. 'Double or quits.'

He took the unused pack from the side of the table and thrust it across towards Ghote.

Without hesitation, without thought, Ghote cut for dealer.

The Rajah cut highest. He won the first hand too, though Ghote had some good cards. He lost the second, quite narrowly, and the third by an even smaller margin. He won the fourth deal thumpingly. Ghote came out on top for the fifth. But it did not matter. The few points the Rajah gained were quite enough to push his total neatly past the hundred mark.

'You don't seem to be terribly lucky, old chap,' he said. 'I'm afraid that's two thousand chips you owe me.'

'Yes,' said Ghote.

It was no news to him.

'Would it be convenient if I let you have the sum tomorrow?' he asked.

'Any time, dear boy. Any time. Though of course I may be fairly busy soon, so on second thoughts you'd better not leave it beyond tomorrow, if you don't mind. I've got a little something in mind which'll take a bit of preparation.'

The even white teeth flashed their unsmiling smile.

'It's rather a nice little something,' the Rajah said. 'As you'll see in due course.'

Ghote got up.

'Shall I come here with the money?' he said.

There were his winnings, of course. But he had little idea at the moment where he was going to get another thousand rupees from.

'Yes, do that. Any time after eleven.'

'Good-bye then.'

He turned and marched stiffly across to the high teak-wood door. As he opened it the Rajah spoke again.

'Oh, one little thing, old boy. When I told you I'd dropped that gun into the sea, that wasn't quite true. I'd meant to. Only someone had the damned cheek to pinch it first. If you do find it, it may turn your luck.'

*   *   *

It took Ghote much less time than he had expected to raise a thousand rupees. He got

132

the sum from the bania who kept a big shop selling food, clothing and a hundred other things at the edge of the big colony of Government Staff Quarters where he lived. He had never visited the man for this purpose before—the very idea had made him walk a bit more uprightly with shoulders a bit more straight—and he had no notion that it would all be so easy.

Diffidently he had asked to see the bania himself, and at once the man—Ghote had never liked him: he smiled too incessantly showing two rows of large, evenly spaced yellow teeth—and at once the man had actually asked if he needed money.

And making loans without a licence was illegal, and he knew Ghote was a policeman. It was too bad.

'Yes,' Ghote had said.

And from then on it was simplicity itself—except that what Ghote borrowed was not 1,000 rupees but 1,200, and what he took away was not 1,200 rupees but 1,200 less a first payment of interest, i.e. 1,000.

With the case of the shot flamingoes in practice wound up, he had taken the afternoon off to go through the grim business of raising the money which he knew would take years to pay back. And now with this unexpected success he found himself at a loose end. Tomorrow he would have the unpleasant duty of appearing before D.S.P. Naik to explain the report he had made out stating that the shootings at the zoo had been the work of the Rajah of Bhedwar but that they had no possible evidence to take to court. D.S.P. Naik would make life very nasty for about a quarter of an hour, and then he would come to realise that there was in fact nothing that could be done. He would give orders to keep the Rajah under observation when there were men to spare knowing quite well that there seldom if ever were. And they would decide on something to say to the Minister. Whatever formula was found would not satisfy the Minister, and he would make a lot of trouble in various ways for a long time to come. But that would have to be borne.

In the meantime Ghote decided to take his son for an outing up to the Hanging Gardens. It was a treat, of a sort, that had been postponed often enough. This afternoon there was at least time for it.

But they set off at odds with each other. Ghote was lugubrious: he could not be otherwise. Little Ved was in tearing spirits: why should he not be?

Still the way he clung to his father's hand and danced along on it like a fire-puppet on a bouncing string soon began to do its work and as they approached the gardens themselves Ghote found he was miraculously shorn of all responsibilities. Later would be a time for troubles; for the next couple of hours at least he could live for what was happening as it happened.

So they ran races, he and his just six-year-old son. Races were the thing with Ved just now. He wanted to do nothing else. They were short races mostly, and Ghote had to take care not to win them. That was understood. They ran from the corner of a flower-bed full of bright-hot canna lilies to railings round a jacaranda-tree in total blue-covered bloom. They ran from a huge poinsettia-tree in a mass of scarlet flower to the railing that edged the tumbling slope down to the sea. There Ghote was allowed to stand for a few minutes, on the plea of old men needing a lot of rest, and stare out at the huge rounded bow-taut stretch of the bay far below. But such employment had no attraction whatever for Ved, and soon enough a new race had to be devised.

'See the mail there, the one with the cane for cutting the grass?'

Ghote pointed to the stooping figure of the gardener about thirty yards away, swishing in regular strokes at a patch of long grass with a thin bamboo.

'Yes, Pitaji.'

'First one to go round him and back to that hedge where it's cut in the shape of a peacock. One, two, three, go.'

This was a longer race and so the winner had to be rewarded with some refreshment. They went over to a coconut vendor, a parched sun-blacked man crouching patiently beside his basket of nuts. Ghote found a coin and the man began the customary elaborate parade of tapping at each fruit with his knuckles to select one jucier than the others and then the sword-sharp knife from his waist slicing off narrow sections of the husk with the nut held firmly against his naked thigh. Ved watched in utter fascination, and Ghote watched Ved, unable to stop himself admiring the set of the boy's head on his neck, the roundness of his young cheek, the deep gloss of his blue-black hair.

And then all of a sudden an odd notion flitted into his head.

Without particularly thinking of the sense or stupidity of it, he began pace by pace creeping backwards out of the boy's sight. And then when he had got about ten yards away and his departure was still completely unnoticed, he turned, ran a few yards and stopped behind the long hedge cut into animal and bird shapes that had been the finishing line of their last race.

He waited crouching there, watching Ved still absorbed as the coconut vendor slipped the razor sharp knife back into his waistband and took in its place a short heavy one and with two expert chops at the hard inner shell cut off the top of the nut. He tore away some still clinging fibres and handed the fruit to Ved, a broad grin splitting his black face.

Ved turned, holding the nut, to his father. And no one was there. The look of dismay on the smooth unmarked face should have been comical. It was blankly disraught.

Ghote leapt up.

'Ved, Ved,' he shouted.

He flung himself awkwardly over the elaborate animal-decorated hedge. He ran forward, still shouting.

It was only a matter of seconds before he had reached the boy, seized him and hugged him hard against his chest. Only a few seconds in which the utter bewilderment had lasted. But the small thin body in his arms was trembling like a struck spring.

The coconut had fallen and the thin juice had trickled out to form a tiny patch of wet stickiness on the gravel and asphalt of the path. It had attracted three flies. After a minute or so Ghote tried to distract the frightened mind in his arms with the offer of a fresh nut. At first Ved simply shook his head in a comprehensive negative. Ghote felt with difficulty into his pocket, and his other arm still hard round Ved's shoulders, and produced another coin, a little too big but what matter? He tossed it to the black-faced vendor who, for value given, went solemnly through his whole performance again.

This time Ved hardly watched.

He took the nut when it was at last offered to him and when coaxed began to drink the sweet liquid. But, though he had now ceased to tremble, he drank without enjoyment. They set off together slowly along the path to the way-out, by mutual unspoken consent.

And all at once, as they did so, an entirely new thought came into Ghote's head from nowhere: what if the person who had stolen the Rajah of Bhedwar's sporting rifle had been one of those he had hoaxed so cruelly?

When the Rajah had so irritatingly added this piece of information to the depressing calendar he had already been given he had simply said, with dignity, that if the Rajah wished to report a theft he must do so to the police station nearest Juhu at Ville Parle. And he had simply put the matter out of his mind. But now it had risen up unbidden, and the more worrying for the amount of time that had passed since he had learnt about it.

Now he had to walk slowly because Ved, in contrast to the way he had come bouncing along at the start of the outing, was walking with drooping sedateness. But at last he saw a shop where he might telephone from. Leaving Ved standing there—and even depriving him of a hand to hold caused him a pang—he plonked down fifteen naye paise, asked if he could use the phone and got through to Headquarters.

First he inquired, with hardly-won casualness, whether anything particular had cropped up. Surely if the Rajah of Bhedwar had been shot there would be talk enough for it to be mentioned in even the most chance conversation. But nothing was said.

He felt chastened. Was he after all being ridiculous? Things did get stolen, in plenty. Why should the Rajah's rifle have been stolen by someone wanting revenge for a cruel trick?

The operator at Headquarters was asking him something. It sounded as if it was for the second time.

'Yes? Yes? What is it?' he said testily.

'Inspector, Sergeant Desai is in the office. He wants to know if you have any orders.'

'Orders? No.'

The idiot. Just like him to hang about the office after he had been pulled off his watch over poor Lal Dass. What did he think there was—

'Hello, hello,' he said into the telephone, suddenly frantic.

'Yes, Inspector?'

'There is something I want Desai to do. Would you tell to go and see Sir Rustomjee Currimbhoy. He is to ask him whether the Rajah of Bhedwar left a sporting rifle at his house. He knows where the house is. Got that?'

'Sir Rustomjee Currimbhoy and the Rajah of Bhedwar. Yes, Inspector.'

The man sounded intrigued. Ghote put down the receiver. He went back to little Ved, who had been standing watching him all this

139

time, his thumb in his mouth as it had not been since he was two years old.

He took him by the hand and with the squidgy wet thumb moistening his palm left the shop. The concerns of a father could not be always sacrificed to the lightest calls of duty, and surely giving this sort of clumsy warning to Sir Rustomjee would be enough?

*   *   *

Even when they had got home Ved was not quite his cheerful self. They ate. Ved fell asleep and Protima took him and put him to bed. Ghote sat on beside the remains of the meal. And nag, nag, nag the little thoughts started to peck away at him.

Say Sir Rustomjee had got hold of the Rajah's rifle in order to kill him? Perhaps it was not such an impossible idea. His life had been wrecked after all. Wrecked by a few minutes of stupid trickery. And those eyes of his. Sometimes they had been screened from everything, sometimes they had been wearily polite, and sometimes . . . had they blazed with a cold fire?

Then he began to think about Desai. He was bound to blunder in the business. If anyone could make that screen sweep up from over the eyes in a sudden fury, it was surely Desai.

The sergeant had a wife, too, and children, four children. He had said he found it hard to provide for them. He attempted to make his barely sufficient pay go further by endless gambling. And nine times out of ten he lost. He had lost to-day, a good deal, over Lal Dass.

Suddenly Ghote jumped up and actually ran across to the telephone. The duty sergeant at Headquarters said that, yes, he had sent Sgt. Desai out as instructed.

'I have been expecting him back for the past hour, Inspector. But you know him.'

'You gave orders for him to report to you?'

'I certainly did, Inspector. With that fellow you have to give orders pretty damn' smart.'

'Yes.'

Ghote put the receiver back quickly. It slipped from his suddenly sweaty palm and nearly fell off the rest. He called urgently to Protima that he had to go out. He sprinted through their little rectangle of garden and into the cool dark.

Getting to Malabar Hill took him an incredibly long time. He had no transport and had to use buses. There were two changes to be made. At each of them the crowds waiting to get on the new bus were thick and sullen. Ghote without hesitation elbowed his way through. The traffic in the streets seemed heavier than ever.

He ran from the bus stop to the Currimbhoy house at a fast trot. He must not pelt full out, he told himself, he might need to be fresh from the moment of arrival.

141

A yellowy street-lamp ahead showed up the big double gate of the house. He recalled from his visit its peeling paint and the scraped gravel of the drive.

A clear picture had formed in his mind now. He saw Sir Rustomjee, tall, upright, wintry-faced, standing with legs firmly apart and the Rajah's rifle in his hands. He heard him coldly utter a sentence of condemnation on moon-faced, blundering Desai. And then the shot. At close range there would be no need to shoulder and aim. It would be just a question of extending the blue-steel barrel and pressing the trigger.

He hurled himself at the big old peeling gate and forced it open. The huge tree beside the house darkened the garden in front to impenetrable blackness. He was forced to make his way towards where he remembered the big front door was almost on tiptoe, hands held out in front of him, his pace dead slow for all the snickers of increasing certainty striking at him in the stomach.

He stumbled over the steps up to the door at last. There seemed to be no lights in the front part of the big old house at all. But the red curtains he had noticed had been very thick. With out-stretched fingers he skimmed over the wall beside the door till he found the big bell push.

He put his thumb on the fat button and pressed and pressed.

9

It was a long time before there was any sign of life in the big old house. But then quite suddenly a light clicked on above Ghote's head and simultaneously the tall front door swung open.

The Goan bearer he had seen before, smart and cosy in his good uniform, was there.

'Police,' Ghote said sharply. 'Where is the sergeant who came two hours ago?'

The bearer bowed slightly.

'You were here yesterday, sahib,' he stated.

'Yes, yes. But my sergeant, where is he?'

'You say he called this evening, sahib?'

The politeness was insufferably calm.

'Yes. I told. Two hours ago. And he has not been seen since. Where is he?'

Ghote pushed past the man into the hall and looked almost frenziedly all round. The big house seemed empty, solid and tranquil.

'I am sorry, sahib. There must be some mistake. No one has called at all this evening. I answer the door always.'

Ghote swung round and gave him a hard look. He seemed confident enough. Was he brazen? It did not look like it.

From behind him a voice spoke.

'It is Mr Ghote, is it not?'

He shot round. Sir Rustomjee Currimbhoy

143

was standing at the head of the stairs, looking down over the heavily carved banisters. He was wearing a dark blue silk dressing-gown which came down to his ankles. From behind him faintly there came the strains of music, European music of some sort, sonorous and majestic.

Ghote felt the heat leaving him.

'Good evening, Sir Rustomjee,' he said, feeling his way. 'I am afraid I am being a trouble.'

'What can I do for you?'

The old man was as distantly polite as ever. Could he, not an hour before, have shot down Sgt. Desai, father and husband?

'Have you had a visit from a sergeant of mine, please?' Ghote asked.

'This evening?'

'Yes. He was making some inquiries about—'

Ghote felt suddenly unwilling to say more. But he plunged on.

'He was making inquiries about a sporting rifle which has been stolen from the Rajah of Bhedwar.'

Sir Rustomjee pursed his lips.

'That young man has gone to pieces in the last year or two,' he said. 'One ought not to allow guns to be stolen. It's one's simple duty.'

Bluff or truth? There was no telling. But in face of such a calm declaration of ignorance from such a respected figure as Sir Rustomjee there was no staying in the house either.

Ghote thanked the old scientist, refused refreshment, muttered more politenesses and left.

He found Desai under the next lamp-post down the quiet street. He saw him from a distance of about twenty yards. He was crouching in the circle of soft yellow light from the lamp playing cards with an old man. Approaching softly, Ghote reckoned that Desai's opponent must be the chowkidar from the big house opposite. Perhaps the very fellow who was meant to have been on watch when the Rajah of Bhedwar had quietly unscrewed the padlock on Sir Rustomjee's laboratory hut.

'Sergeant Desai,' Ghote shouted, breaking the silence of the quiet night.

Desai leapt a mile.

But as soon as he saw Ghote he grinned.

'You know, Inspector,' he said, 'I have been having a run of luck like I never had before. I made up all my losses on that water walk fellow. Imagine that.'

*   *   *

It was more than an hour later when Ghote got back home again. He felt terribly tired and had a thundering headache.

'You are to ring Headquarters at once,' Protima said to him the moment he appeared in the doorway.

For an instant he vowed he would not. How were they to know he had not for some reason stayed away from home all night?

He went over to the telephone. For once he got a connection without trouble.

'Inspector Ghote?'

It was a different duty sergeant now.

Inspector, I have a message, Number One priority from D.S.P. Naik.'

What now? Surely the D.S.P. was not going to try another joke?

'Yes?'

'The Rajah of Bhedwar had been killed. Shot. With a .22 bullet. Out at his shack at Juhu Beach. The D.S.P. says you are to report there immediately and take full charge of investigation.'

*   *   *

It was only when the police truck from Headquarters had pulled up with a shriek of brakes outside Ghote's house, effectively waking all the neighbours, and had started off again with a satisfying roar of its engine that he realised that he no longer owed Bunny Baindur two thousand rupees.

He sat in the front seat beside the driver, a speed maniac who thought of nothing but what fun it was to overtake every other vehicle in sight, and as far as the bucketing of the truck would allow thought over the implications.

146

Of one thing he was sure: he would make no attempt to pay the debt of honour to whoever the Rajah's heirs were. The Rajah had forced him into the bargain: the only person who could force him to pay up was the Rajah himself. And besides nobody knew. That fearsome Sikh servant had been out of the way, and the whole wretched game had taken less than ten minutes.

But had he himself not got a motive for murdering the Rajah? He shook his head to clear the nonsense out of it. Of course he had a motive. But as he had not actually committed the murder, motive did not come into it. And in the meanwhile he was better qualified to find the killer than anyone else. And that was the thing that mattered, he reflected fiercely as the truck took the narrow sandy lane down to the Rajah's shack at about fifty miles an hour. That was what mattered: to get the murderer into the dock.

The door of the bungalow opened in an abrupt patch of white light. A figure issued from it and progressed across towards them at a fast trot. In the headlights Ghote made out after a second or two that it was an inspector of police in uniform. No doubt the man from the local force, M Division.

'C.I.D.? C.I.D.?' the newcomer called out sharply in a yapping voice as soon as he was near enough to be heard.

Ghote dropped down on to the yielding

147

sand beside the truck.

'Ghote here,' he called back. 'Inspector from C.I.D. Headquarters.'

The uniformed inspector came trotting to a halt in front of him, tucking a swagger-stick under his arm.

'Ah, yes, Ghote,' he said briskly. 'Quite right.'

He had a small moustache, not stretching the full width of his upper lip and all brushed severely downwards.

'Inspector Gadgil,' he said. 'I came down as soon as we heard. I think you will find I have taken every precaution, and the chap is locked up in the lavatory. Man on guard, of course.'

'Chap? Lavatory? What chap?'

Ghote had thought his mind had cleared on the way out. He had done his best to shake off his tiredness and prepare himself to tackle the business in a logical way.

'The murderer, of course,' Inspector Gadgil said. 'Thought it best to await your arrival before taking him along to the chowkey here, and the lavatory seemed the most suitable place. Certain problems might have arisen, of course. But you came reasonably quickly.'

Ghote drew in a deep breath. He could smell the salt of the sea in the cool darkness.

'Shall we go back to the house?' he said.

'Certainly, certainly. And I flatter myself you will find everything in order there. The chappie was making a damnable din to begin with. But he has quietened himself down now. Knows we have him, I dare say.'

They took a few silent paces through the soft sand together. Then Ghote ventured another question.

'You caught him red-handed then?'

'Pretty well, pretty well,' Inspector Gadgil answered. Ghote saw the flash of his teeth under the little moustache as he turned towards him. Had he smiled?

'How was that?' Ghote asked.

'The fatality was reported by the Rajah's servant, you know. I myself came back with him here. Great deal to be done in cases of this sort, no use trusting subordinates. And there he was.'

'There? Where?'

'Sitting in an arm-chair looking at the body. Drunk, of course.'

'And the weapon?'

'No trace of that, no trace of that. I put three men on to it at once. Most important to locate the weapon. But no trace at all.'

'But you know it was a .22 bullet?'

In a moment he would have to ask this fellow who his capture was. But, perhaps he would come out with it. If he did not, then he would really be in a good position. He seemed to be not at all the sort of person to let have any advantage, this Inspector Gadgil.

'Yes, yes,' he replied briskly as before. 'The bullet penetrated the heart and passed through the rib cage at the rear. I located it myself on the floor. I did not make the mistake of handling it, of course, but you can take it from me it is a .22.'

'I see. But your man is there on the spot and yet the weapon missing? You are going to be able to connect them?'

'Connect them? Connect them? Naturally. After all when you have the former Palace Officer at Bhedwar who had been dismissed for inefficiency come creeping back and you find the master dead, there is hardly any other conclusion.'

Ghote took this in and rapidly considered it. But it was too much to handle.

'The former Palace Officer?' he asked, throwing away whatever advantage he had had.

Inspector Gadgil stopped on the threshold of the big bungalow.

'Yes,' he said. 'That only came to light after I had rung Headquarters. This fellow Captain Harbaksh Singh was Palace Officer out at Bhedwar in the old days. In the former Rajah's time.'

'I see,' said Ghote.

He smiled to himself. By chance the authority of the C.I.D. man had been preserved. Then he frowned. What Gadgil had told him did not sound as if it altogether added up. And if it did not . . . Gadgil did not look like a man who would happily surrender a pet

150

theory.

'Shall we go in then?' he said.

'I will lead the way,' Inspector Gadgil said. 'I have a pretty accurate idea of the scene.'

He went, short, important steps, in ahead of Ghote, through the hall and into the room where that terrible game of gin rummy had been played.

The card-table was no longer there. Doubtless it had been folded up and put away somewhere. Ghote was glad of it. But otherwise the room was as he remembered it. Large heavy pieces of teak furniture everywhere, the side-table with the same array of bottles, the golden air conditioner humming away still, cool though it was.

The french windows on to the veranda were open, and just inside them lay the body of Bunny Baindur, Rajah of Bhedwar. He was lying on his back, with his arms extended as if he had been flung down. In his chest the entrance wound of the bullet had ploughed a wide hole. Ghote recognised the aperture at once: he had seen almost the identical wound not three days earlier. In the body of a red flamingo.

'Now your Elan Harbaksh Singh was sitting just here,' Inspector Gadgil said, pointing with his swagger-stick to one of the heavy arm-chairs which was turned to face the open windows.

He gave his little moustache a twitch of

satisfaction.

'I do not think he counted on us getting to the scene quite as quickly as we did,' he said. 'But I know how to move snappily when the need arises. Yes, indeed.'

'And when you found him?' Ghote asked, proceeding fatedly step by step to a conclusion that loomed larger and larger.

'Asked him what he was doing,' Inspector Gadgil replied sharply. 'Saw what condition he was in, and asked him pretty damn' quick to account for himself.'

'What did he say?'

'Nothing that made any sense. So I put two and two together and had him locked up in that lavatory inside two minutes.'

'Inspector,' Ghote said, 'I would like to question him now. Would you be so good as to have him brought in?'

'Certainly, certainly. Though I hardly think you are going to get anything out of him. Nerves all gone to pieces, you know.'

'I see,' Ghote said.

Gadgil trotted over and began to bark orders at his men on guard over the locked lavatory. He appeared to have to bark quite a lot of orders, but at last he came back in.

'On his way,' he said. 'On his way. Now we will see what we can get out of him.'

He took up a stance in front of the drinks table, his swagger-stick clasped firmly at either end across his stomach.

Ghote went over to him.

'Inspector,' he said, 'I must request that you do not intervene during my interrogation.'

Inspector Gadgil gave one single twitch to his little brush of a moustache.

'I think you can rely on me, Inspector,' he said. 'Yes, I think you will not find I commit any breaches of etiquette.'

The door opened and Captain Harbaksh Singh was marched in by two constables.

He was a man of sixty or more. This was the fact that stood out about him, all the more because he so evidently attempted to look a young forty. He held himself militarily upright, but with effort. His moustache was youthfully rakish, but well sprinkled with grey hairs. There was nothing he could do about his paunch of a belly or the heavy mottled flush on his cheeks.

'Captain Harbaksh Singh?' Ghote said. 'My name is Ghote. I am an inspector of the Bombay C.I.D.'

Captain Harbaksh Singh's bloodshot eye fastened on him.

'Ah,' he said. Then you're just the chappie I want to see. What I want to know is: what the hell do your fellows mean by locking me up in that lavatory?'

'Please be seated, Captain Singh,' Ghote said, with a coldness designed both to pull the ground from under this aggressive figure and to reassure Inspector Gadgil and thus keep him happily quiet.

For a moment it looked as if his tactics were going to fail. Gadgil had clutched at his swagger-stick in open fury at the invitation to the captain and the captain himself made no immediate attempt to sit. But the crisis evaporated. Gadgil slowly took notice of the chill in Ghote's tone, and the captain quite suddenly subsided with an audible groan into one of the arm-chairs.

'I understand,' Ghote said to him, 'that you were on the scene of the crime when my colleague here arrived.'

A prim little flick of a smile appeared on Gadgil's face. Captain Singh slowly raised his eyes to Ghote.

'Yes,' he said. 'I was. Want to make anything of it?'

'It is not a question of what I want to make out of it,' Ghote said sharply. 'It is a question of what a magistrate may make out of it in due course.'

Captain Singh shook his grizzled head under its neat white turban.

'Won't wash,' he said. 'Won't wash at all. I'd only just got here a couple of minutes before all those policemen of yours came rushing in, and young Bunny had been shot half an hour or more earlier.'

'And how do you know that?'

Ghote cracked in with the question with all the speed of a courtroom drama merchant.

But he failed to discompose the young-old figure slumped in the heavy chair.

'How do you think I knew? When I saw the young fool lying there, what do you think I did? I looked to see what was wrong with him. Thought he might be drunk, though he could hold a phenomenal amount of liquor.'

'And you found he was dead?'

'He was dead. And he had been dead some time. I fought in a war once, you know.'

'Ah, an experienced witness,' Ghote said, infusing a sudden pleasure into his voice. 'You could be most helpful. Tell me, did you form any opinion about how close the killer was when the shot was fired?'

Captain Singh looked over at the flung-down form of the Rajah of Bhedwar.

'I should say he was shot with a rifle, from a fair distance.'

'And how do you know that?'

It was Inspector Gadgil. Ghote's move to soften up his witness had produced an unexpected side-effect.

He swung round from Captain Singh and gave his uniformed colleague a long, cold look. It took a second or two to make its effect, but then it penetrated.

'Oh, your pigeon, Inspector, your pigeon,' Gadgil muttered.

Ghote turned to Captain Singh again.

'Yes,' he said. 'As far as we know the Rajah was shot with a rifle from a distance. Where

155

were you earlier this evening, Captain Singh?'

Captain Singh's bloodshot eyes brightened considerably.

'Until ten minutes before I got here I was at the Sunny Sands Hotel a little way along the beach here,' he said. 'And I was surrounded by good friends every minute of the evening.'

Ghote swung round and looked Inspector Gadgil full in the face. The tightly clutched swagger-stick actually dropped from his hands.

Ghote went and sat on the neighbouring massive teak arm-chair to Captain Singh's.

'So much for the immediate circumstances,' he said. 'But I have an idea you could be most helpful to my inquiries in other directions.'

He blatantly stressed the 'my' and saw from the glare Captain Singh promptly gave the still very disconcerted Gadgil that the point was taken.

'Of course, old boy. Anything I can do to clear up this messy business,' the Rajah's former Palace Officer said. 'It so happens,' Ghote said, 'that I have recently had certain dealings with the Rajah.'

Out of the corner of his eye he noticed a further degeneration in the collapsed state of Inspector Gadgil.

'From what I saw of the Rajah,' he went on to Captain Singh, 'I would say he was a man who would have had many enemies. But I would be grateful if you, who knew him well, could tell me without prejudice who might

156

have wanted to kill him.'

Captain Singh had been staring at the spreadeagled body as Ghote had been speaking. Now he turned his bloodshot eyes full on him.

'Nobody I can think of could have possibly wanted to kill Bunny Baindur,' he said.

10

In the spacious, heavily furnished room in the Rajah of Bhedwar's Juhu Beach 'shack' with the wide open french windows letting in the quiet sound of the sea running up the wide stretch of the sands and with the body of the Rajah lying knocked flat by the bullet which had killed him, Inspector Ghote found his mouth had positively opened wide with surprise.

He looked at the paunchy figure of the Rajah's former Palace Officer, Captain Harbaksh Singh, sitting in a slumped attitude in the big teak chair opposite him.

'Nobody?' he repeated stupidly. 'You are saying that nobody would want to kill the Rajah?'

'Nobody I know,' Captain Singh said. 'And I knew his set well enough. Inside out you might say.'

'But—'

Captain Singh shook his grizzled young man's head.

'Nobody would want to kill Bunny Baindur,' he said. 'And I'll tell you why.'

Ghote leant forward.

'Nobody would want to kill him because Bunny had never cared a damn about anybody.'

'Yes,' Ghote said, 'I know he felt like that about people. But surely if he treated them as dirt there must be a lot of people who would have wanted perhaps to kill him?'

'No,' answered Captain Singh with complete assurance. 'No. You see, he cared for people less than that. He did not care for them enough to want to hurt them even. He cared for nobody, not at all.'

Ghote thought about this. He knew on the one hand that it was not true: Bunny Baindur had cared enough about the people he had played his joker's tricks on to select with deadly accuracy what would hurt them most. On the other hand a man in Harbaksh Singh's position would know a very great deal about a person they had served like the Rajah. A palace officer meant a palace: a palace meant intrigue and intrigue meant the need to know.

He looked over towards the open french windows and the rapidly cooling body of Bunny Baindur.

'You seem highly certain,' he said to Harbaksh Singh.

'I got drunk with his father when the boy was born,' the captain said. 'It was my duty. I taught him to use his first gun. I made the necessary arrangements for his first dancing girl.'

'And you say he cared for nobody?'

'He cared for his father. And his father died when he was ten. He never cared for his mother. The palace women began to gossip about it when he could hardly walk. He has no close relatives. He never married. He had hundreds of affairs, always with some sort of dancing girl. They never lasted a week.'

'Relatives?' Ghote said. 'Do you know then who inherits the title?'

'No one,' said Captain Singh. 'It was part of the terms of the Instrument of Abdication when the State was made over to India. There was to be no Rajah of Bhedwar after this one, and no income for any successors.'

'Who will he leave his money to all the same?'

'There won't be more than a few rupees to leave, old man. Bunny spent every penny of his income and he'd eaten up all the capital by the time he dispensed with my services.'

'Yes,' Ghote said, 'and why did he do that?'

The battered young-old captain smiled. Crookedly.

'Look at me, old boy. What use do you think I'd be to Bunny Baindur? I was lucky he hung on to me as long as he did. And that was pure forgetfulness.'

'Lucky? You liked him then?'

'Liked him? No, you couldn't like something that was as incapable of human feelings as that boy. No, I was lucky he kept me on because I'm fit for nothing else.'

He looked down at the spreading heap of his stomach jutting out in front of him as he sprawled on the big chair.

'And why did you come here to-night?' Ghote snapped out.

He put the question fiercely not because he expected to catch Harbaksh Singh out. It did not sound as if his alibi would fail. But there was a need to say something, and quickly.

Harbaksh Singh rolled his bloodshot eyes towards Ghote.

'I came to see if I could borrow a few hundred rupees,' he said.

Ghote pounced.

'From this man who cared for nobody? I think you have been telling a pack of lies, Captain Singh.'

But Harbaksh Singh was not to be shaken. He shook his head wearily. The grizzled hair under the neatly wound white turban.

'He might have lent me something,' he said. 'Or he might not. He didn't care enough about me to refuse, and he didn't care enough about all the things I've done for him since he was three or four years old to agree.'

It was convincing. Ghote felt so passionately

160

curious about its implications that he would have put his next question whether it had been useful or sensible or not.

'What would you say if I told you that in the last six months this man who cares nothing either way for anybody had gone to an immense amount of trouble to play certain expensive practical jokes on certain people, choosing with infinite pains just what would hurt them most?'

It took Harbaksh Singh some while to take it all in. He sat in the big chair opposite Ghote, slumped almost as if he was asleep. But in due time he did reply.

'I would never have believed it.'

But there was a small frown on his time-marked forehead under the white turban.

'Of course,' he went on slowly, 'I have not seen him more than from a distance for the last six months and more. It is nearly a year since he dismissed me.'

The frown was still there, persistent as a midge.

'There is something,' he said, teasing the words out. 'Something.'

Then he sat up straight, with an echo of his first, hard-kept militarism. He looked intently at Ghote.

'Yes,' he said, 'I would believe you. There was always something there, deep, deep down. I refused at times to think about it. But I knew really it was there. I wonder what started it

161

off?'

Ghote looked at the sprawled corpse.

'I would be most surprised if we ever knew,' he said.

*   *   *

Sgt. Desai reported to him in his office early next morning. He was all eagerness. A moon-struck magnet looking for iron. Ghote, after a night of supervising police surgeon, fingerprint men, photographers, ambulance men, looked at him grimly.

'Where do we go, Inspector? Who's the first suspect we see?'

It stung Ghote more than he expected.

'How do you think a murder inquiry is conducted?' he shouted. 'Do you think the officer in charge just sits making up theories and goes rushing off accusing one person after another?'

'No, Inspector,' Desai said, looking like a bullied schoolboy.

Ghote glared at him. He stood in front of his desk totally silent.

'You do not think that, do you?'

'No, Inspector.'

'Then what do you think?'

'Don't know, Inspector.'

Gritting his teeth, Ghote made himself reach down to his drawer of scrap paper and take out a wad. He picked up a pencil. He

162

wrote, 'Death of the Rajah of Bhedwar' at the top of the first sheet.

He looked up at Desai, who had tiptoed—every creak of his boots maddeningly audible—over to the heavy little chair against the wall and was sitting on it now, face vacant as ever.

'At least we know this,' Ghote said. 'Murder is not a joke. Nobody kills a person as a joke. You have to be serious, if only for a short time, to commit a murder, to take a human life.'

He paused, his thoughts hesitating.

After a few seconds Sgt. Desai leant forward on his heavy chair.

'Yes, Inspector,' he said reverently.

'Damn it,' Ghote shouted at him. 'Do you think I have nothing better to do than to spend all my time thinking about what causes people to kill other people. The way to deal with a murder case is to find out who had the opportunity to kill the victim, where he was killed and when and exactly how, and then the identity of the killer is often plain enough. And *bas*. Enough. Make sure of every step of your evidence and get him into court.'

'Very good, Inspector.'

Desai, idiot Desai, actually began to rise to his feet as if he was going off at once to carry out the orders given.

Ghote slammed his open palm down on the surface of the desk in front of him with a resounding bang.

'None of which helps when your man was shot from a distance, in a place where in the middle of the night there is hardly anybody about, ever.'

'No, Inspector.'

'You know the only thing that has come into my head?'

'No, Inspector.'

Those wide, wide stupid eyes.

'It is this: that almost anyone could have shot him and that no one—no one—had any reason to except those people he had made victims of his damned jokes.'

'Yes, Inspector.'

Desai licked his thick lower lip.

'Who's the first suspect we see, Inspector?'

*   *   *

Anil Bedekar, sometime street urchin, owner of last year's favourite for the Indian Derby, was not exactly willing to be interviewed, especially as Ghote thought it wisest only to say he wished to see him 'in connection with the theft of the racehorse Roadside Romeo.' It took half the morning to get him to the telephone to discuss making an appointment at all.

'I cannot see. I am at stables.'

'But I could come to your stables, Mr Bedekar.'

'Come to Poona to talk a matter that is

164

finished?'

Ghote gulped a little.

'But certainly to Poona, sir.'

'All the same, I am very busy.'

'Perhaps I could come early, sir? Early tomorrow? Before you have other engagements?'

'Early?'

'Yes, Mr Bedekar. I would come as early as you wish.'

There was a long pause at the other end. Tiny, nearly audible conversations flickered to and fro. Ghote began to wonder whether he had been left hanging on to a mere nothing.

'Mr Bedekar?' he said tentatively.

'Very well, Inspector. You can come.'

'Thank you, sir. It is most kind. What time shall I make it?'

'I am up at four, Inspector, to watch the gallops. Come then.'

'At four, sir?'

'Yes, man. Four. Four a.m. See how you like that, Inspector.'

Ghote had not much liked it. It had meant waking in the middle of the night to drive the hundred and twenty miles to Anil Bedekar's stables just outside Poona and arriving there as the very first grey light began to seep into the sky. It was cold—not just pleasantly fresh, but cold. And this was something that Ghote had not taken into consideration. He shivered as he approached the low range of white buildings where once a horse called Roadside Romeo had set off to take the Indian Derby for his owner and had come back all unknown when his place had been usurped by a donkey.

But if Ghote was unprepared for the cold, Sgt. Desai was ridiculously struck down by it. He marched along half a pace in the rear and his teeth chattered. Loudly.

'Stop that damned noise, man,' Ghote snapped at last.

Before the sergeant had time to enter on any long explanation, Ghote tapped sharply on what seemed to be the main door to the buildings.

It swung open with a jerk that took him entirely by surprise and he found himself staring into the ominous twin barrels of a steadily held shotgun.

'Good morning,' he said.

He spoke quickly, to get some unprovocative words out as soon as possible. He tried not to speak too quickly, so as not to send out dangerous waves of nervousness.

'What do you want?' said the man holding the gun.

He was a square-faced, grey-haired fellow of sixty of so, dressed, for all the coldness, in cotton shorts and a flapping-tailed raggedy shirt. But, in spite of the poorness of his clothes, he looked as if he well knew how to use the expensive shotgun in his hands. And at a range of four feet his pronounced squint would hardly affect the issue.

'I am wishing to see Mr Bedekar. By appointment,' Ghote said.

He had been on the point of adding his name, but a last moment thought made him hesitate. A police officer is not popular everywhere.

Without moving the gun by so much as a millimetre and without taking his squinting gaze off Ghote's own face, the grey-haired man called out: 'Says he wants to see you, sahib.'

From somewhere inside the building a voice Ghote recognised as Anil Bedekar's shouted back.

'Wants to see me? At this time—Wait. Ask him if his name is—Oh, I do not know what. Ask if he is police inspector.'

'Inspector Ghote from Bombay,' Ghote called back.

He heard Anil Bedekar laugh. It sounded like a hyena, even though there was a grudging note in it.

'Let him in,' he called.

The pointed gun curtly waved both himself and the anxious-looking Desai into the building. A warm smell of horses and straw assailed his nostrils, and he was grateful for it.

Anil Bedekar, short, pock-faced, carelessly dressed was standing among a small knot of men peering intently at a horse. Ghote saw that Jack Cooper—once a suspect as the

167

joker—was among them together with a jockey holding a round white racing helmet loosely in one hand and two attendant syces, one holding either end of a rope bridle round the horse's head.

'Inspector,' Anil Bedekar said as he caught sight of him, 'how do you like getting up early in the morning?'

'If I can just have ten minutes to talk that matter,' Ghote answered, 'I do not mind.'

But Anil Bedekar had turned back to the horse.

'Perhaps, perhaps,' he answered in a distant voice.

Ghote stood and waited. Desai, standing a little behind him, was looking round at the warm stalls, each with its thoroughbred in it, with an air of dumbstruck wonderment. But it was a long wait. The group round the horse in front of them talked in low voices and in a jargon Ghote hardly understood. He gathered that something seemed to be wrong with the horse and that it was a question of whether it was permanent or temporary, but what exactly it was he could by no means make out.

After a while he noticed a gentle moaning sound from behind him. He turned. Desai was no longer dumbfoundedly wondering. He was propped up against a much-stained white wall behind them, sound asleep.

And then a sudden decision was taken. Almost before Ghote realised it, the horse that was the centre of discussion was being led outside by the two syces and the others were going with it. Ghote shook himself and followed. He took one look at Desai and decided to leave him where he was. If he was given a pretty sharp awakening, so much the better.

Outside it was still cold. Anil Bedekar and Jack Cooper were wearing thickish trousers and coloured windcheaters. Ghote's trousers were deplorably thin and his jacket no better. He flapped his arms vigorously. The nervous thoroughbred started and reared up a little. Anil Bedekar swept round and gave him such a furious glance that he thought his chances of an interview without creating a lot of fuss must have come practically down to zero. Making every effort to move with perfect discretion he tiptoed after the rest of the party.

The horse was put through a severe test on the gallops. Time and again it made a short timed sprint. After each one there was much consulting of stop-watches and discussion. Even when at last the sun began to appear over the horizon and the mists to lift a little it was still very chilly. Several times Ghote had sneezed. Each time he had successfully stifled every bit of the noise.

And then after one sprint which seemed no different from the rest there was sudden jubilation. Jack Cooper slapped the little jockey on the back as he slipped out of the saddle. Even Anil Bedekar himself came up, unslung a Thermos flask from its strap over his shoulder and offered tea all round. Ghote was included. As the racehorse owner poured the delicious-looking steamy liquid into a plastic cup for him he looked at him humorously, stumpy teeth bared in a grin.

'Well, Inspector,' he said, 'you are cold. You have earned your ten minutes of talk.'

'Can we step aside a little?' Ghote said.

Anil Bedekar's good humour persisted.

'If you like. If you like.'

They walked over the dew-wet grass together. When they were just out of earshot of the others Ghote opened his interrogation. He made his remark sound as casual as he could.

'I am afraid we have both lost a friend,' he said.

Bedekar glanced at him quickly.

'You mean the Rajah?' he said. 'I saw it in the paper. But I do not know that he was exactly a friend.'

Ghote would not let the quick hope that sprang up at these words take fire. Perhaps Anil Bedekar did not feel that the Rajah was a friend. But all the same if he had killed him he was not going to go about telling everybody he hated him.

He proceeded cautiously.

'Not a friend?'

Anil Bedekar grunted.

'Who am I?' he said. 'I am Anil Bedekar who began life in the gutters of Bombay. That is where I was born. In a gutter. And what was he? A rajah. A prince.'

'And the last of the Rajahs of Bhedwar,' Ghote said.

'Yes, yes,' Anil Bedekar said, joining with decent gusto in the mourning. 'The last of his line.'

He left a little silence in the chilly air. Then he laughed. Loudly.

'And I am the first of my line,' he said.

Ghote looked over at the substantial white-walled stable buildings.

'You have certainly come a great way,' he agreed.

'And a little further only to go now,' Bedekar said.

Ghote guessed what he had in mind. The one more step, the final ambition, the Indian Derby.

'A little further?' he asked innocently.

'Yes,' Bedekar said. 'I am determined to win the Indian Derby. You know something?'

Ghote turned to look at the racehorse owner. His pocked face was shining with a sort of innocent enthusiasm.

'You know something? It is my heart's desire to win that race because that was the first race I ever saw. I was eight, maybe nine years old at the time. How should such a man as I know when he was born? Horoscopes are

171

for the respectable. But I was eight or nine and, I do not to this day know why, I went up to Mahalaxmi Racecourse that day. Perhaps it was the crowds that drew me. Where there were crowds there was a little to eat for a hungry boy, and I saw the Indian Derby. And that was what did it. That was what made me say for the first time "Push". And ever since have I pushed. And now it is only very little push more.'

Ghote saw his chance.

'But last year,' he said. 'Last year when you had it in your pocket?'

And the cheerfulness did drain away from the pug-ugly face.

'Last year,' Anil Bedekar said, 'When that happened to me I was so angry I would have killed the person who did it. With my hands I would have killed.'

Ghote saw that his broad, short-fingered hands were even now convulsively clutching.

'But at the time you had no idea?' he asked.

Quite quietly.

'At the time I had no idea.'

Anil Bedekar drew in a long breath of the crisp morning air.

'And now still today I have no idea,' he said.

'You are certain? No clue? No suspicion even?'

'None. None at all. But now I do not worry.'

Ghote looked at him keenly. It was impossible to tell what was going on behind that not pleasant countenance. 'Did you try to find out yourself?' he asked.

'For a day or two. But soon I saw it was no good. The job was too well done.'

'Yes,' Ghote agreed. 'It was well done. It must have been done by a person with great resources.'

'Yes.'

'And by somebody who knew you well?'

'Yes. That also.'

'And you thought of no names even?'

Anil Bedekar walked over the wet grass in silence for a little, thinking.

'No,' he said. 'I could not think of a single name.'

Ghote decided it was time to play another card.

'Not even the name of the Rajah of Bhedwar?' he said.

Anil Bedekar came to a complete halt. He looked at Ghote hard.

'What are you telling?'

'I asked if you had thought it was possible the Rajah was the one responsible for that joke.'

'No,' said Anil Bedekar decisively. 'You are wrong, Inspector, if you think that. Yes, he was rich. He could have done it. He had the money. And, yes, he knew me and my habits quite well. But, Inspector, there is something you have not thought.'

'What is that?'

173

'Inspector, a man does not rise from the gutters of Bombay to be leading owner year after year without being able to tell things about people. That is what you have to know. What the people you are facing would do. And I tell you this: the Rajah of Bhedwar did not care one pice for me. He did not care enough to joke me even.'

'That is what I would have thought,' Ghote replied, looking steadily at the racehorse owner. 'But towards the end of his life that man did begin to care. To care about playing his jokes. And the day before he died he confessed it to me.'

Anil Bedekar thought about this. The lines on his squat brow were twisted in plain thinking.

'Inspector,' he said. 'That too was one of his jokes. That confession. He told me he had joked you already. He made you bet more than you wanted on a horse that was not a chance. Cream of the Jest.'

'But it won,' Ghote said.

'By a big mistake. And that time the joke was on the Rajah.'

'The joke was on him both times,' Ghote said. 'He did not confess till I showed him I knew all about him.'

'And you were going to prosecute? Was it suicide?'

Anil Bedekar's mind was quick.

'No,' Ghote said. 'We had not enough

evidence to prosecute. But if I had come to realise who the joker was, someone else could have done also. It was murder.'

He was taking in every detail of the racehorse owner's appearance. Looking for the least tell-tale sign. A change in breathing rate. A tap of the foot. A clenching of the fingers. However slight.

But there was nothing.

And that meant nothing either way.

He decided he would have to put down yet one more cautious card.

'Did the newspaper account you read tell you very much about the circumstances of the Rajah's death?' he asked.

'That he was found dead the evening before, in his shack at Juhu Beach only. And that foul play was suspected,' Anil Bedekar replied.

Ghote saw that he was going to have to begin the patient process of feeding the racehorse owner suggestion after suggestion about the killing, hoping that at one answer he might betray more knowledge of the circumstances of the death than he ought to know. But for this time was needed, and it was hard to be sure how much time Anil Bedekar was prepared to give him without his making a fuss and thus warning his man to take care.

He had a start.

'Yes,' he said, 'the local police called me out to Juhu and I arrived—'

He stopped short.

Away in the low range of stable buildings a sudden high, sobbing, extraordinary howl had shattered the early morning calm. By his side Anil Bedekar swung round. Fifteen yards away the group round the heavily breathing horse turned sharply. But Ghote ran.

He ran full pelt towards the stables and he cursed himself at every pace. That howl could only be Desai, and heaven knows what had happened to him. But the man with the shotgun was not in the party out with the horse, and he had looked as if he would have no hesitation in using the gun. There had been no shot so far, but with an idiot like Desai in a blind panic you could never tell what might happen. The crack of a shot and the thud of pellets entering a solid body might come at any moment.

11

Not a sound came from behind the closed door of the stable building as Ghote reached it. He seized the door knob and twisted it hard. The door remained obstinately closed. Ghote took a step back and surveyed it. It was not particularly solid. He might be able to break it open. He must be able to. To have Desai shot because of a whim of his own, because for a joke he had left him asleep there, wouldn't bear thinking about.

He swung round, marched five paces away, turned and charged.

There was a sharp rending sound as his shoulder came into biffing contact with the door at the exact point for maximum leverage. The flimsy affair flew wide open.

In the empty stall where the horse at exercise had been stabled an alarming sight met his eyes. The squinting man with the shotgun was lying flat on his back in the dung-melded straw on the floor. The gun was across his throat and holding it firmly with one hand at the end of the barrels and the other on the stock was Desai, solidly astride the squinting man's chest.

For several seconds Ghote stood and stared while his mind tried to grapple with the startingly reversed situation his eyes told him existed. Behind him Anil Bedekar, Jack Cooper and the jockey came curiously up.

Ghote quickly shook himself free of his perplexity.

'Well, Desai,' he said, 'were you having trouble?'

Sgt. Desai turned his head a little, after having given the helpless man underneath him a glare of warning.

'This chap tried to hold me up with that gun of his, Inspector,' he said. 'He told I was a racing spy.'

'But why should he have thought that?' Ghote snapped irritatedly.

'You came in with me. He knew that.'

A sheepish look spread over Desai's dark face. 'Inspector,' he said, 'let me tell you the truth.'

'Certainly.'

'I fell asleep, Inspector.'

'I know that, you idiot.'

'Well, Inspector, when I woke up I found I was all alone, so I thought anyway, in Mr Anil Bedekar's stables.'

'Well?'

'Inspector, what a chance. I thought I could find enough hot informulation to last me months. Inspector, I have to keep a wife and children on my betting, you know. What else could I do?'

From behind Ghote Anil Bedekar jumped forward.

'And what the hell did you find?' he shouted.

He was extremely angry.

Desai's face went doubly anxious. He scrambled off the prone body of the squinting man and got awkwardly to his feet.

'Mr Bedekar, sir,' he said. 'Not a damn' thing. That was the worst part.'

Ghote swung round.

'Never mind that, Mr Bedekar,' he snapped out. 'Just tell me where you were on the evening that the Rajah was shot?'

For a moment two emotions, anger and curiosity, struggled for mastery on Anil Bedekar's face. Ghote glared at him and his anger with poor Desai was chased from the field.

'So Bunny Baindur was shot?' Anil Bedekar said reflectively.

Ghote registered the mark up to innocence, and discounted it almost as quickly. Bedekar was no innocent in other ways. This would not have been the first big bluff of his life.

'Yes,' he said to him, 'the Rajah was shot. During the evening. Where were you then?'

'I was here, of course.'

'In the stables?'

'At my house on the other side of the road.'

'And could you prove that?'

Ghote had little doubt that he could, and he felt all the exasperation of coming to the end of a promising trail. But it was a fact that people like Anil Bedekar did not spend the evening at their own house all alone. There would be servants by the dozen who would have seen him, and whose evidence could be cross-checked till it was pretty well proven. There would be friends for dinner by the dozen too, no doubt.

'No, Inspector,' Anil Bedekar said, with calmness. 'I cannot prove I was in my house.'

'You cannot? But why?'

'Inspector, at this time of year as often as not I am up at three or four in the morning. I

179

am getting on in age, Inspector, I need my sleep.'

'So you go to bed early?'

'Often very early. Very early indeed when poor Bunny Baindur was shot.

'And no one can prove you were in bed?'

'Not absolutely, Inspector. I could have got out of my own house unobserved if I had wanted.'

Anil Bedekar stood looking at him quietly, almost insolently.

*　　*　　*

The drive back to Bombay seemed interminable. The truck got hotter and hotter. Ghote's head, thick from the lack of sleep the night before, began to thud. He gave Desai a turn at the wheel. It was not a success. When for the fourth or fifth time the truck wandered squarely into the middle of the road, along which other vehicles were apt to be coming at speeds of up to seventy miles an hour, Ghote ordered him tersely back into the passenger's seat.

Nevertheless when they got to the city centre he did not take the turning towards Headquarters. Desai, sitting grinning away amiably to himself, looked round.

'Hey, Inspector, you took the wrong way.'

'Did I?'

'Yes, Inspector.'

The earnest solemnity simply fed the fire of Ghote's fury like generous pieces of dry fuel being dropped one by one on to the sulky heart of a fire. In a moment they would blaze into life.

'Oh, yes, Inspector. To get to H.Q. you have to turn left just back there. It won't be easy to do now, Inspector. This is a no-through road here.'

'I can see a sign as big as that for myself, thank you.'

'Yes, Inspector. I thought as you missed the way once you might not be driving so well just now, Inspector.'

'I did not miss the way.'

'Oh, but yes, you did, Inspector. You ought to have taken that left turn back there. Going to be very difficult to get out of this, Inspector.'

He began craning all round, looking at the state of the turbulent city traffic.

'It is not going to be difficult,' Ghote stated flatly.

'Oh, but yes, Inspector, to get to H.Q. when you missed the turning from here is not easy.'

'We are not trying to get to H.Q.'

The look of surprise on Desai's face was exactly what Ghote had expected. Why then, he asked himself, did it make him so doubly furious?

'Oh to hell, man,' he snarled. 'We are going to interrogate Lal Dass, of course. This is a

181

murder inquiry: not a chance to drink tea in office.'

'No, Inspector. I mean, yes, Inspector.'

*   *   *

Lal Dass, the hathayogi, had had his ashram, crowded with disciples, at the sea-shore up beyond Wore. Everybody knew that. It had been endlessly repeated in the papers. Where exactly it was, Ghote did not know. But he reckoned that all he would have to do was to inquire.

As soon as they got near to the sea he stopped the truck, leant out and shouted at the first person he saw, a solid grey-haired grandmother voluminously wrapped in a dark green sari.

'I am looking for Lal Dass.'

That should be enough. It was.

The serious, solid face under the tightly drawn harsh grey hair split wide open in a monster grin. The stout old lady laughed till she had to wipe her eyes. It was a long time before she could talk.

'Only now you are looking,' she spluttered.

'Yes. I am looking now,' Ghote said.

He had the feeling that the laughter was directed partly against himself for looking for Lal Dass at all as well as against the discredited hathayogi.

'Yes, I am looking,' he said. 'And I am police

182

officer.'

The grandmother wiped her eyes with the corner of her sari.

'Police officer, is it? You are going to arrest? Good. My son-in-law he lost fifty naye paise over that man.'

'Where can I find?' Ghote said, more sharply.

The stately green-clad figure pointed.

'Down there till you come right to the sea,' she said. 'And then along to right. You will see where they all had their tents when they believed in that fool. And now there is one tent only.'

Vengeance darted from her solid face. Fifty naye paise, half a rupee, that was real money.

Ghote let the clutch of the truck in with a jerk.

In less than two minutes they were down at the beach and there, true enough, were the signs of a recently numerous tent colony, dirt, mess and rubbish scattered generously. And past it all, up against the rough grey stones of a short section of sea-wall there was one tent left—if tent it could be called.

It consisted of a single sheet of coarse sacking held to the top of the wall by four or five heavy stones and supported at the lower end by two crazily angled bamboo sticks. Even from a distance it was possible to see the whole interior. It consisted solely of a large water-jar and Lal Dass.

The hathayogi was sitting cross-legged on the sand, his head bowed, his plump figure motionless. Ghote stopped the truck. He turned to Sgt. Desai. Somehow he could not contemplate this sight with that bumbling figure standing at his elbow. Before he knew it the fool might fling himself on the hathayogi the way he had flung himself on Anil Bedekar's squint-eyed syce.

'Sergeant,' Ghote said, 'take a good look at where we are, and then go and find the nearest telephone. Ring in to Headquarters and let them know where I am. All right?'

Desai sat in the passenger seat of the truck and the various parts of Ghote's orders passed one by one over his moony countenance. At last he came to the end of them.

'Okay, Inspector,' he said.

'And when you come back,' Ghote added, 'just wait nearby till I see you.'

'I come back?' Desai said.

'Yes, you come back. You go and telephone and then you come back here, which is why I told you to take a good look at where we are. And you tell me if anyone at Headquarters had any messages also.'

'Oh, I see now, Inspector. Yes, sir. I would do that.'

Ghote waited. Desai sat where he was.

'Then go,' Ghote said quietly.

'Oh, go? Yes, go. I see. Then bye bye, Inspector.'

And he did go. Ghote watched him marching away along the dirty sand and turning out of sight with a wondering air. It would take him a good deal of time to locate a telephone. There should be long enough to get what he could out of Lal Dass.

He walked slowly over the sand towards the sea-wall and the pathetic awning. Four or five yards away he took care to kick at an empty, battered tin lying in his way. He saw that it had once contained something called Cocoa Maltine. It made a satisfactory clatter. Lal Dass did not so much as move a muscle.

Ghote walked on right up to the edge of the tent. Still the hathayogi did not move. Ghote altered his position a little so that his shadow fell squarely across the scuffed up sand in front of the plump man's eyes.

And then he did look up.

'You have come for my advice, my son,' he said.

It was no sort of a question.

With great graciousness Lal Dass gestured with his right hand at the sand in front of him under the shade of the awning.

'Sit, sit, my son,' he said.

Ghote weighed it up for a moment. Then he ducked down under the awning and sat cross-legged in front of the hathayogi. He noticed, with a faint sense of surprise, that he looked no different than he had when he had seen him across the smooth water of the tank

185

waiting to begin that feat of levitation that had ended so ignominiously. His light brown skin was still as smoothly shining in the plump folds across his belly. His loin cloth still looked as fresh and white and uncrumpled as it had done on that day of days when the press of half a dozen foreign countries and the complicated rig-out of the television cameras, not to speak of thousands of his fellow countrymen, had waited for his least move. His smile was still as gentle, as placid, as benign. His brow was as unfurrowed.

'No,' Ghote said sharply. 'No, I have not come for advice. I have come for information. You are speaking with a police officer.'

The hathayogi inclined his head half an inch to the right in gentle acknowledgement, but said nothing.

Ghote began again.

'I have come to investigate the trick that was played on you,' he said.

Lal Dass looked over at him and smiled. It was a smile of simple serenity.

'Why do you do that?' he asked.

'An elaborate hoax was played on you by someone,' Ghote said. 'It is our duty to discover who. Have you any idea yourself?'

He leant forward ready to memorise each word. One slip, one wrong emphasis and he might have a clue as to whether Lal Dass knew the Rajah and knew that it was he who had so cruelly humiliated him.

Lal Dass was smiling still.

'It is finished,' he said softly. 'Why must you think of it still?'

'But he tricked you, made a fool of you before thousands of people, television cameras even.'

'He did not make a fool of me, whoever he was,' Lal Dass said. 'It was I who made a fool of myself.'

For a moment Ghote was nonplussed. There was too much of truth in what the hathayogi had said for one thing. But he recovered quickly enough.

'It is not a question only of you looking a fool,' he said. 'A great deal of public confusion was caused. A great deal of money was wasted.'

'Wasted?' the plump figure in front of him said musingly.

'It was lost,' Ghote replied with sharpness. 'A great many members of the public lost large sums owing to this ridiculous hoax.'

'Yes,' said Lal Dass.

He lapsed into silence for a little.

'Yes,' he repeated at last. 'It is good for them to lose money. We must all lose money.'

'All—'

The fluting, gentle voice went on.

'We must all lose all the money we have. That is the way.'

Ghote shifted uneasily. It was not that the soft sand was uncomfortable underneath him.

187

'I know that these must be your views,' he said stiffly.

'No,' said Lal Dass.

'No, they are not your views?'

'They are not my views: they are the way.'

Ghote began to feel some exasperation. He welcomed it. With a steam-head of annoyance he could ride over the uneasiness that such religious talk always produced in him.

'If members of the public lose sums of money through the activities of some joker,' he said, 'then that is police matter and must be investigated until a satisfactory conclusion is reached.'

But his sharpness did not seem to impinge on Lal Dass. The plump, smooth-skinned hathayogi simply smiled again.

'Yes,' he said, 'whether it is money or police it is the same thing.'

Ghote saw well enough what he was getting at.

'I do not understand,' he said, with great stiffness. 'You must try to,' Lal Dass replied.

The patient tone tipped Ghote over the edge into real irritability.

'All right, I do understand,' he barked. 'I understand quite well. You are saying that the world ought to be able to get on without money and without policemen. You are saying that to someone who is a policeman.'

'Yes.'

The gentle statement. Ghote had not meant

to get involved in this sort of argument. But he leant forward determinedly now.

'You think that just because I am a policeman,' he said, 'that I am incapable of thinking for myself. That is the mistake all you people make. I may not think about the role of the policeman very often, but let me tell you I have thought about it, and having thought I am very happy to stay as police officer.'

Lal Dass smiled. He smiled his smile of distant, bland unbelief.

'No,' Ghote said, as if the word was a heavy spear he hoped might penetrate the thick armour.

He looked at the smoothly shining uncreased face in front of him.

'No,' he said, 'a world without money, a world without crime, a world without police— all that is just too good to be true.'

'The good is the true, my son.'

Ghote fought back a sharp temptation to snap that he was no son of anybody but his own dead father.

'You are not listening,' he said instead. 'You will not pay attention. That is your trouble, the trouble of you and all like you. You will not pay attention to what is, what really is, around you. There is crime in the world. It is no use saying only there is not. There is. And when you have crime it is better for everybody that you have policemen to stop it.'

Lal Dass's smiling face kept its gentle

189

meditative expression, as Ghote had all along known it would.

'And if it is the other way,' the hathayogi said calmly. 'If it is the police that bring the crime?'

'But it is not,' Ghote replied, unfoxed by this. 'That is the unreal world. In the real world you have crime, and policemen to stop it if they can. And you have to live in that real world.'

'No,' said Lal Dass simply. 'You do not.'

'You did not,' Ghote retorted.

'I did not?'

'No,' Ghote said, no longer doing anything to make life easy for the man who had been hoaxed. 'No, you let yourself be made a public fool of by real tricksters in this real world.'

Lal Dass considered this in silence for a little while. His plump body stayed as absolutely still as it had done from the first moment Ghote had sat in front of him under the scanty shade of the awning. Ghote, once more, shifted a little in the soft sand. Then Lal Dass spoke, gentle voiced as ever.

'Perhaps I was tricked,' he said.

'Yes,' Ghote said, taking off the pressure now, 'I am sorry, but you were tricked. Can you tell please just how it happened?'

Again Lal Dass considered in silence. Would he speak, Ghote wondered. Or would he seize on the chance to say nothing, and, if indeed he had been responsible for the death of the Rajah of Bhedwar, avoid the risk of giving himself away?

And under the shade of the awning on the sun-hot beach the silence grew.

12

At last Lal Dass gave Ghote another smile of benign sweetness.

'Yes,' he said, gently as the tiniest breeze, 'yes, I will tell.'

Ghote held his face impassive. He dared not wonder what it was that had induced the hathayogi to speak rather than to drift off on some long, happy meditation—or to pretend to do so. But he was going to speak. And if he was not what he seemed, if he was a man of passions who had been intolerably insulted and had taken his revenge, then something might show through. He listened intently.

'People came to me,' said Lal Dass. 'Once people came. Now they do not come. But they came once. First in twos and threes, then in dozens, at last in hundreds.'

The gentle voice ran down to nothingness and silence fell again under the hot awning.

'Go on,' said Ghote quietly.

'Soon I did not know who they were the ones who came, and soon I did not know even who were the ones that stayed. It did not seem

191

to matter. They listened to what I had to say.'

The placid eyes resting on Ghote seemed to note the tiny expression of cynicism he had been unable quite to keep from flitting on to his face.

'Oh, yes,' Lal Dass said gently. 'There is not much in listening, I know. But I knew too that sometimes, even against the will, sometimes something lodges there and cannot be removed.'

Ghote wondered at the deep-down astuteness the hathayogi had shown in pulling him up so quickly. Was it a sort of genuine spiritual shrewdness, or was it a man trying the first feint in a long wrestling match?

He wanted for Lal Dass to continue in his own time. And soon enough he did so.

'They had watched me,' he said. 'They had watched the growing signs I was able to give of mastery over this body of ours. They knew I fasted. None better: they ate the food that was given to me. And they saw that the fasting did me no harm.'

Ghote glanced involuntarily at the glowing, golden belly so close in front of him.

'Yes,' Lal Dass said, speaking quickly for him. 'Yes, I fast still.'

Again Ghote was aware of the alert mind. Of the man fighting for his life? Of the saint?

'And then,' Lal Dass resumed, 'when I suggested that one day I would walk on water as a test of my growth there was much excitement. Soon there was much talk about it. And then they asked me to try.'

Lal Dass stopped.

'They suggested to you the tank you should try on?' Ghote prompted.

'Yes. One day they took me to the tank, very early in the morning. They asked me to try.'

The large glistening eyes fixed on Ghote with a new brighter light.

'I tried,' Lal Dass said, 'to show them I could not do it. I thought it would be a lesson for them.'

He lowered his head.

'And you succeeded?' Ghote asked.

'Yes. I walked on the water of that tank as easily as I could walk across a smoothly polished floor,' Lal Dass answered.

And then for the first time that Ghote had noticed a small frown crinkled the smooth, baby-bland serenity of his brow.

'I was not happy,' Lal Dass said. 'I was not happy that it had happened before I knew I was ready. But I could not think how it had happened if I was not ready. No other explanation came to me. I did not even know where to look for one.'

'And did you know that there was so much public interest in the feat you had tried and were to be asked to perform again?' Ghote said.

'No,' Lal Dass replied.

And almost immediately he added

something.

'Yes,' he said. 'Yes, I did know. I paid little attention to all the talk of all those people. But I did know. It had become something that I knew. And I found I had agreed. And I thought: perhaps someone, one only, will think about what he sees. I did not go back.'

'And you never suspected then that you were being set up as victim of a huge hoax?' Ghote said, making no attempt to soften the bluntness.

'No,' Lal Dass answered.

'Do you know the Rajah of Bhedwar?' Ghote said next.

'No.' replied the hathayogi simply.

'He was shot,' Ghote said. 'Do you ever go out to Juhu Beach?'

'No.'

Again the simple negative.

Ghote abandoned this attempt at shock tactics.

'You say you never suspected about the hoax at all,' he said. 'Why was that?'

'I was too worried.'

'Too worried?'

'By what had happened already,' Lal Dass explained calmly. 'By finding myself walking across the tank when I should not have been able.'

'And this worry,' Ghote asked, 'did it lead you to look more carefully at the people who had persuaded you to do what you knew

194

should have been impossible?'

'I paid them less attention even,' the hathayogi answered. 'I was concerned with myself.'

'And then came the day of the great walk,' Ghote prompted him before he could go off into more introspection.

'Yes. Then came that day. And I thought: if I have done it once I can do it again. I tried to prepare myself for it.'

Ghote changed his position a little in his soft hollow of sand, and put a question that was off the strict line of his inquiries but which he could not help asking.

'Did you get yourself to a full state of preparation?'

'No,' Lal Dass answered without hesitation.

He thought for a moment and then added an explanation:

'No, I did not get myself prepared. I am far away from that. But what I did was to persuade myself that I was truly ready.'

'And you were made a laughing-stock,' Ghote said.

'Yes.'

There was nothing to be learnt from the simple syllable. Ghote tried a new tack.

'I had gone from the tank before you recovered consciousness,' he began.

Lal Dass moved then. He leant forward two or three inches.

'It was you,' he said.

195

'Me?'

'You were the police inspector they told me had pulled me from under the water.'

'Yes, that was me,' Ghote said.

'It was a good action,' Lal Dass replied.

His limpid eyes beamed at Ghote.

'It was doing my duty,' Ghote replied. 'Doing a policeman's duty in the real world where sometimes people are found drowning.'

Lal Dass moved his head in a gentle negative.

'It was a good action for this world,' he said. 'But if you had not made it, nothing would have been different.'

'You might have been dead,' Ghote said.

'Yes, I might have been dead. What of it?'

'You were ready to die then?' Ghote asked.

'Yes, I was ready to die.'

'You were shamed enough to wish to be dead?'

'Oh no. I am always ready to die,' Lal Dass replied, with it seemed a twinkle of humour. 'Always ready to move to the next phase.'

Ghote was rattled a little by the rebuff.

'Very well,' he said. 'But when you did regain consciousness, what were your feelings then? You felt anger?'

'No. Why should I have felt anger?'

A spun of irritation sprang up in Ghote's mind.

'You should have felt anger because someone had made you look the biggest fool

Bombay has seen for years,' he said, his voice beginning to rise to a shout.

'But it does not matter to me what people think about a thing like that,' Lal Dass replied with the blandest calm.

Ghote sat and considered. He had lost, certainly. From this wrestling bout he must retire defeated. But that did not mean that there might not be a way of catching his man yet. Unless . . . unless his man was not the man he suspected at all, but in truth the figure he gave himself out to be.

A black, heavy bar of shadow fell across the yard of scuffled sand between himself and Lal Dass. Ghote looked up. It was Desai, standing stiffly to attention. And grinning.

'Well, what the hell do you want?' Ghote snarled.

'Message from H.Q., Inspector. Damn' urgent.'

He stood there, still grinning, waiting.

'If it's urgent, man you had better tell, isn't it?'

Ghote lunged to his feet. His back just caught the edge of the sack awning. One of the bamboo stakes came out of the sand. The awning flopped down till it rested against the hathayogi's left shoulder. He did not stir. Furiously Ghote picked up the stick and began pushing it into the yielding, hopeless sand.

'Well, man, well?' he barked at Desai.

'There has been request for you to report in

person to Ministry of Police Affairs, Inspector. D.S.P. Naik say you better get there *ek dum.*'

The bamboo stick would not stay upright. Ghote knelt on the soft sand, seized it with both hands and jabbed desperately. He felt the sweat springing up.

'Please to leave it.'

It was Lal Dass's gentle voice.

'I will not,' Ghote shouted. 'I knocked it down and I will put it back if it is the last thing I do.'

He jabbed again. The bamboo flopped lurchingly sideways once more.

'But leave it,' Lal Dass said. 'Ten or twenty times a day boys knock it down as a joke. Perhaps it would be best to leave it altogether.'

'No,' Ghote snorted.

Once more he drove the short, bendy pole in with all his force. And this time it did stay. He leapt to his feet.

'I must go,' he said. 'Business. Important business.'

He almost ran along the sliding slippery sand back to the truck. And he was unable to prevent himself noticing that before he had reached the vehicle the bamboo stick had fallen once more.

Driving through the turmoil of traffic towards the imposing new building of the State Ministry of Police Affairs and the Arts, Ghote felt a solid thundercloud of tiredness building up inexorably at the back of his head. He knew

198

that in fact he had been lucky: more often than not a murder investigation meant forty-eight hours without sleep to begin with, covering the ground fast before any trails got cold. But he had at least seen his bed for a few hours the night before. The ground to be covered in this case was so small in extent that all the routine work that could be quickly done had been done in hours. And had produced nothing.

So he ought not to have been too tired. But he knew why suddenly now he was having to fight off that overwhelming sensation: it was the prospect of appearing before the Minister himself. And especially as he did not really know what would be expected of him.

He brought the truck to a careful halt outside the huge, white smooth-walled building in Mayo Road. He left Desai, whom he had simply and firmly ordered to stay silent, sitting despondently in the passenger seat. He climbed the long wide steps and entered the great pillared and marbled entrance hall.

And the moment he gave his name to the tall, magnificently turbaned chaprassi who reigned over these, wide spaces he knew that things were not good. The man's eyes instantly brightened.

'Yes, Inspector,' he said vigorously. 'This way, if you please.'

And he led him with brisk, military steps into the high-corridored interior of the vast building. Somebody, plainly as could be, meant business.

The chaprassi flung open an outer office door without ceremony. A secretary, an Anglo-Indian girl in a short skirt, all brazen efficiency, sprang to her feet.

'Inspector Ghote,' the chaprassi announced impressively.

The girl sank back on her swivelling typist's chair, bent to her intercom box and pressed a discreet button.

'Inspector Ghote,' she announced respectfully.

A voice, mangled and incomprehensible, said something in reply.

'Would you go in at once please?' the girl said to Ghote.

The chaprassi himself, well over six foot six of muscled body, swept forward, opened the door at the far end of the outer office and held it wide.

Ghote gave himself one quarter of a second to straighten his back and marched forward.

'My dear Ganesh.'

Behind an immense desk, dark glasses heavily framed in white, smart suit beautifully laundered and plangent tie shining, was Ram Kamdar.

Ghote, nerved up for a personal Ministerial reprimand of the first order, was completely silenced.

'But take a pew, take a pew, old boy,' Ram Kamdar said.

He bustled round the huge desk and shifted by half an inch a low, springy-looking little arm-chair placed in front of it for visitors. Ghote, as much to give himself time to adjust as anything, slowly sat down.

'Cigarette?' said Ram Kamdar.

He seized from the glass surface of the desk a large, elaborately carved box (support indigenous craftsmen) and pushed it towards Ghote.

'I—I do not smoke. I am sorry,' Ghote brought out.

'First-class decision,' Ram Kamdar said, making his way back to his own plump chair behind the desk. 'First-class decision. All the statistical evidence is firmly behind you. Nothing has a greater risk-bearing element than smoking.'

He took a cigarette and flipped a flame from a tiny gold-plated lighter.

'Well now,' he said.

'It is you who want to see me or the Minister?' Ghote asked.

'Oh, you're to see me. The Minister only likes to be presented with an appropriate end-product. And before he is given that a certain amount of idea-orientation will probably be necessary.'

'Yes?' said Ghote.

'Yes. The presentation format is always of prime importance, especially when we're dealing with top echelon. It might be vital for me to build up a climate of acceptance before any factual items were brought forward.'

Ghote thought he grasped the point. He waited.

'That's why I was so anxious to get hold of you, my dear Ganesh. You realise I simply haven't the information to base any motivation study on?'

'You mean,' Ghote asked, determined to be clear before he embarked on any answer, 'you mean you do not know anything about that joker business?'

'Precisely. Not a thing.'

Ram Kamdar smiled with a great flash of white teeth.

'Well, it is quite simple,' Ghote said. 'You know of course that the Rajah of Bhedwar has been shot?'

'I heard that you were on that case, when I was in touch with your Headquarters on a routine conditioning mission. But I wondered whether this was a mere sub-function, or whether it indicated the other business had been brought to a conclusion.'

Ghote shook his head clear.

'The fact is that the Rajah was responsible for the jokes,' he said. 'He shot the Minister's flamingoes.'

'Oh, good work,' Ram Kamdar said, looking patently surprised. 'The Rajah, eh? Now who would have guessed it?'

'Unfortunately,' Ghote went on, 'we could

not obtain the necessary evidence to bring a successful prosecution.'

'Ah, probably better not in any case,' Ram Kamdar said. 'Much better not, I'd say. Could cause an altogether unwanted shift in environment.'

'Yes,' said Ghote.

He looked at the P.R.O., leaning happily back in his plump chair, puffing idly at his cigarette. He appeared to be in a reflective mood. Ghote began wishing he was over at Malabar Hill talking to Sir Rustomjee Currimbhoy. The joker business was finished now.

'Yes,' Ram Kamdar said, musingly, 'we shall have to ponder just how this altogether novel element in the situation is to be presented. There are tricky considerations here and there.'

Ghote began to push himself out of the low arm-chair.

'Well, that is your job, I suppose,' he said. 'And I have—'

'No. One moment, my dear fellow. Your help may be necessary. This situation has at present a high novelty-factor for me. Until I've made a bit of a motivation study I don't know whether there'll be anything more I'll need to know.'

Ghote resigned himself to a wait. But he wished all the same that he was at this moment in that preserved, dark-shaded drawing-room in the Currimbhoys' old house.

Ram Kamdar stubbed out his cigarette in a heavy brass ash-tray, also dedicated to the encouragement of some branch of handcraft. He reached for the big carved box and pushed it towards Ghote, with a lift of an eyebrow behind the tinted glasses.

'Thank you, I do not smoke,' Ghote said stiffly. 'No. No, of course not. Do you mind if I do?'

'Certainly not.'

A tiny sweat of impatience sprang up on Ghote's tensely held palms.

Ram Kamdar lit up and savoured a deep puff.

'Now the situation as I see it,' he said, 'is this: we know now who was responsible for that act of wanton destruction which so properly enraged the Minster, and—'

He paused, propped his cigarette in the ash-tray and went off on a new tack.

'Old Bunny Baindur,' he said. 'Extraordinary. You're quite sure?'

'I am perfectly convinced. But there is no possibility of obtaining formal evidence,' Ghote stated.

'Old Bunny, eh? There certainly weren't any behaviourial indications. I knew him, you know. Only the merest acquaintanceship, of course.'

'We met in his party at the water-walk,' Ghote said.

'Oh, yes, so we did. So we did.'

Ram Kamdar leant forward across the glass top of his huge glossy desk.

'That water-walk,' he said, 'was that—'

'Yes,' Ghote said, 'it was. And now, Mr Kamdar.'

He stood up.

Ram Kamdar stood up. But he waved Ghote down.

'Now, it's Ram, my dear fellow. Ram. We agreed on it, my dear Gopal.'

'Ganesh.'

'My dear Ganesh. Now please sit down and help me out on this one. What we must get is a clear consensus before I even think of going to the Minister.'

But Ghote did not sit down.

'I regret,' he said. 'I have been assigned to a murder inquiry. Full-out work is absolutely necessary. I must go. Now.'

Ram Kamdar looked shocked behind the big white-framed dark glasses. Ghote turned on his heel and walked straight out.

*   *   *

When Ghote got out to the truck again it was to be greeted by a studiedly woebegone Desai. He made up his mind to ignore him. No doubt he was resenting being told to sit tight and keep his mouth shut. But there were limits to the amount of tactfulness it was possible to show to a subordinate. It had to be made quite clear that his heavy-footedness simply made him unsuitable for almost every task that might come his way.

'We are going to the Currimbhoy house now,' Ghote said flatly. 'I shall have to question Sir Rustomjee. You will stay outside in the truck. I may need you later, in case a question of checking alibis with the servants arises.'

Desai gave him a long look.

'Well, man,' Ghote snapped, 'have you understood those simple instructions, or not?'

'Yes, Inspector.'

Ghote started the engine and eased the truck forward to the edge of the maelstrom of traffic in Mayo Road.

Desai coughed. He coughed very loudly. If he had held up a placard with the words 'Please listen' scrawled on it, he could hardly have signalled to Ghote more clearly.

Ghote leant forward and peered at the jostling stream of cards, bicycles and lorries.

Desai coughed again.

'Bloody traffic,' Ghote said. 'If you do not grab your first chance you can be stuck here for hours.'

Desai fell silent. But not for long. They still had not got out into the road when he spoke.

'Inspector.'

'Quiet, man. Surely you can see I am looking at the traffic?'

'Yes, Inspector.'

So he wants sympathy, Ghote thought savagely. Well, he can want. I have better things to do just now than to make things nice and comfortable for someone who does not deserve it.

A tiny gap appeared in the stream of cars in front. Ghote took his foot off the clutch and surged forward. The truck got its nose out into the roadway and stalled.

'Damn,' Ghote snapped.

He tugged at the starter. The truck failed to respond. Oncoming cars had to halt. Behind them drivers started banging at the sides of their vehicles. One incautious individual even used the forbidden horn.

Like magic a traffic policeman appeared, yellow cap jammed on his head, buttons hard rubbed till they glinted, blue trousers sharply creased, black sandals gleaming with polish. He was all ready to enjoy himself with a torrent of abuse.

Then he saw who it was causing the hold-up. His face fell.

Ghote got the engine to life. The jam he had created had at least ensured him a clear run on the other side. It was not the direction he had meant to go but he took it.

'Going round a back way then, Inspector?' Desai asked, with immense interest.

'I am going to the Currimbhoy house,' Ghote said icily.

From the corner of his eye he saw the woebegone look had come back to Desai's dark face with renewed intensity. Well, let him look. If all he could think of to say was a fatuous remark like that, then silence was infinitely preferable.

He swung round the corner to get back to his route to Malabar Hill. And there, spreadeagled right across the narrower road, was a huge lorry from the back of beyond somewhere with 'Public Carrier' on a board over the cab and the driver and his cleaner out in the roadway staring up at their monster in bewilderment.

Ghote braked and quickly stuck his head out of the window to see what was happening behind him. What was happening was that a little stream of traffic that had followed his truck evidently in the blind hope that it was on to a good way of dodging a jam, was piling up in the narrow road. There was not the least chance of turning and extricating himself. He glared at the huge bulk of the lorry at right angles to them.

Desai laughed, a silly, sort of choked laugh.

'Just by the rear entrance to our own building, Inspector,' he said. 'Way in to the canteen.'

'Suppose you get out and start putting the fear of God into those two, Sergeant?' Ghote said in his most biting tone.

Really, when things had gone wrong, to start

making idiot remarks about the Headquarters building.

Dolefully Desai jumped down and began shouting at the men in charge of the huge lorry. They, of course, promptly began shouting back. And it became clear almost at once that the driver, a little slightly hunchbacked man in a torn but very gaudy shirt and dirty brown shorts, was a great deal more expert at a slanging match than poor, confused Desai.

Ghote thrust his head out of the window of the truck again.

'All right, Sergeant,' he called. 'Let them get on with it.'

Desai seemed glad of an excuse to retreat.

'Yes, sir, Inspector,' he shouted as if he was in charge of some giant parade and had just been asked to move off by the right. He marched back to the truck and climbed in with a patently ridiculous air of dignity.

Ghote sighed and turned away a little to indicate that he was not going to join in a conversation however much Desai wanted.

The sergeant did, for once, get the point. He sat in silent gloom.

Then, noisy as a shunting engine in the shut-off quietness of the driving cab, Desai's stomach began to rumble. It rumbled loud, long and continuously.

And at once Ghote realised what the trouble had been: the man was hungry. He had

had no lunch, and it was late. Come to that, he was really pretty hungry himself. And he had put all Desai's hints down to a need for a little conversation.

He turned to him now.

'Come on, Sergeant,' he said. 'As you point out, we can be up in the canteen from here in less than a minute. Sir Rustomjee can wait half an hour.'

It was the nearest to an apology he could reach.

13

It was, in fact, more than half an hour before they set out for the Currimbhoy house on Malabar Hill once again. Ghote encountered D.S.P. Naik. It was just as he was leaving the canteen. The D.S.P. unexpectedly came bustling along the corridor towards him. He ought to have been at his own lunch. The lunches of D.S.P.s did not take place in the canteen and they did not last just half an hour. But instead here he was. Ghote would have preferred not to have seen him: since he had had Sgt. Desai foisted on to him in that extraordinarily irresponsible way he had developed a resolve to steer clear of D.S.P. Naik in any and every way he could.

He tried to pass with a distant nod of

respectful greeting.

'Ah, Inspector,' the D.S.P. said, pouncingly.

'Yes, D.S.P. ?'

'Just the man.'

'Yes, sir?'

No escape now. The D.S.P. was looking at him hard. But perhaps this was to be only an inquiry about his health. D.S.P. Naik was notorious for the morbid interest he took in other people's bodily afflictions.

'Case going all right, Inspector?'

That could be parried all right.

'Yes, D.S.P. Still a lot of work to do, however. I am just going to interview Sir Rustomjee Currimbhoy.'

A crumb of hard information always was useful. The D.S.P. looked vague as soon as he was given it: he plainly did not want to get further involved.

'And your sergeant, Inspector?' he said. 'Er-what's-his-name?'

'Sergeant Desai, sir,' Ghote replied, allowing himself a touch of grimness.

'That's the chappie. Making good progress?'

Suddenly Ghote decided to take the bull by the horns.

'No, sir. No, D.S.P. I regret he is not. I had meant to speak to you, sir, on the subject as soon as opportunity arose. To tell the truth, sir, I find him a hindrance in my duties.'

The D.S.P.'s round face with its little tab of soft black moustache went more and more distant with every word. By the time Ghote had finished he might have been at the other end of a long telephone line. And from this distance a small dry voice spoke.

'It's your duty, Inspector, to see that the men put into your care are given some responsible training. I don't allocate you a sergeant solely to let you take the weight off your feet: I place a man under your guidance so that he can learn the ropes. And if he fails to do that, Inspector, I shall want to know the reason why.'

And the D.S.P. turned on his heel and stamped away.

*　　　*　　　*

It was only ten minutes later when, with Desai softly humming a film song in the truck beside him as they ran rapidly towards Malabar Hill, that Ghote realised that the D.S.P. had been coming towards him when they had met in the corridor. If that was so, why had he turned and left in the other direction? The answer must be that he had a bad conscience.

And the sole result of that had been that he himself had got into the D.S.P.'s bad books.

'Sergeant,' he said, 'I trust that appalling humming sound will cease when we go into the house?'

'But I thought you want me to stay outside, Inspector.'

'Very well. If you come into the house.'

Ghote brought the truck to a halt, and this time he made the brakes scream.

When the same Goan bearer he had seen before opened the front door to his ring he thought he detected the faintest expression of disapproval on his face at this noisy arrival. He brusquely asked to see Sir Rustomjee.

He did not have long to wait in the cool, dim, stiff-with-furniture drawing-room, shaded and dark even in the afternoon glare, before Sir Rustomjee appeared.

'Ah, my dear Inspector,' he said. 'Is there anything I can do for you?'

To Ghote, watching him with all the alertness he could muster, he appeared not a whit different from the earlier occasion they had met. He decided to try the same tactics he had used with Anil Bedekar.

It is a small thing only, Sir Rustomjee, and I was doubtful even about coming, since the last time I was here was with the Rajah of Bhedwar.'

Sir Rustomjee's grave face remained calm.

'That was certainly a terrible affair,' he said. 'Tell me, has your department come to any conclusions about it?'

'Nothing which I know about,' Ghote replied. 'Had you heard the full circumstances?'

Sir Rustomjee shook his head in courtly negative.

'I simply read a short account in the paper,'

he said.

All right, Ghote thought, we will try our little test.

'It is all a mystery still, I believe,' he said. 'He was there in the grounds of the Sun 'n Sand Hotel, Juhu.'

Sir Rustomjee was listening intently, but not the faintest sign of surprise or disagreement disturbed his long face with the deep-sunk eyes.

'Was it some sort of assault?' he asked. 'One hears these stories of goondas lying in wait for people they suspect of carrying large sums.'

There was nothing at all to indicate whether this was the concerned question of a polite man or a calm bluff. Ghote sighed inwardly.

'No,' he said. 'It was a case of shooting. The Rajah was shot at from a distance and killed.'

'I see,' said Rustomjee gravely. 'What sort of a weapon was this then?'

And there was perhaps something in the tone of the question that did not quite ring right. Sir Rustomjee seemed to know the answer too much. But it was difficult to be certain about such things. He was after all a man of unfailing politeness.

'The weapon seems to have been a light sporting rifle,' Ghote replied.

'Oh, yes?'

And this time Ghote was certain that, even in the quiet light of the big furniture-filled room he had seen Sir Rustomjee's right hand, thin and long-fingered, tense for a single moment.

Then the Parsi scientist smiled a little.

'But what was it you wanted to see me about?' he asked.

'It is still the matter of the hoax that was played at your laboratory,' Ghote said.

Sir Rustomjee stiffened. If there had been doubt over his reactions to talk about the Rajah's death, there could be no doubt about this reaction now.

'Inspector,' he said, 'I do not wish to be discourteous. But, quite simply, I have said all I am prepared to say on that matter.'

Ghote stiffened.

'I must remind you that there is such a thing as Article 179 of the Indian Penal Code,' he said. 'It is offence to refuse to answer a public servant authorised to question.'

Sir Rustomjee's long, oval face took on its look of unflagging politeness.

'My dear Inspector,' he said, 'let us sit down and discuss this like reasonable men.'

He indicated a high-backed, red plush-covered chair. Ghote sat. But he would not let himself sink back into the creaking, comfortable depths. Sir Rustomjee, however, lowering himself into a similar chair nearby, crossed his legs in apparent comfort.

Ghote returned to his questioning.

'Sir Rustomjee, can you tell me if there was ever anyone whom you suspected as being the perpetrator of that senseless joke?'

The blank screen over the deep-set eyes seemed to harden. But Sir Rustomjee considered the question with care.

'No,' he said at length. 'No, there was no one.'

'You thought about it at the time?'

'Yes. Yes I did.'

'And some name, or names, came into your mind?' Sir Rustomjee shook his head.

'No,' he answered. 'At first, naturally perhaps, the question "Who had done this to me?" presented itself burningly enough. But at every turn I came up against a complete blank, and very soon I realised that there was no point in asking the question. I came to the conclusion, in fact, that I must put the whole thing out of my mind.'

He smiled. The winter smile of a piece of statuary.

'That is why I was disinclined to go into the matter again with you, Inspector,' he said.

Ghote bowed his head in some acknowledgement.

'Unfortunately there appear to have been other people involved in similar incidents,' he said. 'It is for them that my investigation must continue.'

'And you are making some progress?'

There was a sudden note of wariness in the old man's voice. Ghote forced himself to betray no sign that he had detected it.

216

'Yes,' he said cautiously. 'Yes, I think I can say that I have made progress.'

'And—'

But Sir Rustomjee stopped himself.

'My dear Inspector,' he resumed almost at once, 'you must forgive me. I am becoming a deplorable host. Will you take some refreshment?'

Ghote smiled a little.

'No, thank you, sir,' he said. 'I hardly feel I am guest. This is an official visit.'

Sir Rustomjee inclined his white-haired head.

'But all the same,' he said, 'a glass of lemonade?'

'Thank you but I must not stay long,' Ghote said.

He waited for a little hoping that the old scientist would go back to whatever it was he had been going to say when he had interrupted himself. But he guessed it was a forlorn hope. The old man plainly would like to know more about how far the investigation had proceeded. And equally plainly he had decided not to ask.

Ghote went back to his former line of questioning.

'You were saying, Sir Rustomjee, that you did not at the time the incident occurred have the least idea who might be the perpetrator. But may I ask if you have subsequently formed any conclusions?'

217

He waited for the answer like a hunter lying up on a machaan with a goat tethered at the foot of the tree below. He did not expect the answer to be a simple "Why, yes, I suspected the Rajah of Bhedwar," but he did hope that the manner in which it was given might betray something.

'No,' said Sir Rustomjee evenly. 'No, as I told you, I have attempted to put the whole business right out of my mind.'

There was nothing in the words to indicate anything. But the old man had paused, paused just a little long, before saying them.

It was not much to go on. It might be only the chance effect of a hundred and one considerations that had nothing to do with the case a spasm of indigestion even, the sudden remembering of another engagement, anything. But it was enough to make Ghote move on to the next stage in a now familiar process with a little more confidence.

'I told you my investigations had made some progress,' he said.

And again the wary flicker of interest appeared to reveal itself. Ghote longed to stride to the windows and push back the heavy red curtains to their utmost, to jerk aside the shading blinds. He would have liked to have had Sir Rustomjee under a glare of lights so as to detect the least tell-tale muscular movement. But he must continue to operate in the cross-shadowed gloom that he found himself in.

'In fact,' he went on, 'I think I can tell you that there is little doubt who was responsible for that hoax.'

Now quite clearly Sir Rustomjee was forcing his face into a rigid blankness. There was nothing more to be gained by teasing him.

'Shortly before the Rajah of Bhedwar's death,' Ghote continued, 'he admitted to me that he alone was the figure behind your affair and several others. Does that surprise you?'

It certainly had not appeared to have done.

Sir Rustomjee sighed gently.

'Yes,' he said slowly. 'Yes, it does surprise me. My brother and I knew his father well in the old days. It was one of the most conservative princely families of India.'

'So I understand,' Ghote replied. 'But I believe also that the young Rajah was the very last of the line, cut off from all ties.'

'Yes, that is so. I begin to see how it was possible that he did the things you mention. You are sure that it was he?'

'You begin to see,' Ghote replied. 'Tell me, please, what is it that makes you see?'

Would Sir Rustomjee reveal a process of reasoning that he had in fact made much earlier, made while the Rajah was still alive?

'I can—That is—Well, I scarcely know.'

Sir Rustomjee, for the first time since Ghote had known him, was completely at a loss.

'But you told you saw why the Rajah had

219

fooled you,' Ghote said sharply.

It was a mistake. Sir Rustomjee sat more straightly in his big red arm-chair.

'Really, Inspector,' he said, 'it would seem from your tone that you think you have a right to pry into my mental processes. I note that you have discovered who played that trick on me. But as I said earlier I am doing my best to put the whole thing out of my mind. So I cannot exactly thank you.'

He pushed himself to his feet, his long thin body slightly bent.

'And now I think I must ask you to leave,' he said. Ghote stood up in his turn. But he did not make any effort to go.

'I am prying into your mental processes, Sir Rustomjee,' he said. 'And the reason is simple. We are not certain why the Rajah of Bhedwar was shot, and it is at least highly probable that he was shot by someone he had played a cruel trick upon.'

He expected a blaze of cold fire at this. But Sir Rustomjee actually smiled.

'Inspector, it was stupid of me not to see that at once. But, to tell you the truth, my mind recently has not been working as it should. The edge is dulled, Inspector.'

Ghote refused to let himself show any compassion. If Sir Rustomjee had been bowled over so badly by the trick the Rajah had played on him, then he was all the more a possible murderer.

220

'Sir Rustomjee,' he said, 'I must ask you to account for your movements on the evening of the day before yesterday.'

Sir Rustomjee looked at him.

'And that is why you are here, is it, Inspector?' he said. 'I see you have been a little disingenuous.'

It was a high-faluting word, and one which Ghote was never quite sure of the meaning of. He wondered whether Sir Rustomjee had chosen it half on purpose, to put him meanly at a disadvantage. But he knew what the general tenor of the remark had been.

'A police officer has certain duties,' he said, very stiffly. 'He has to consider the best means of carrying them out.'

'My dear Inspector, I perfectly understand. I—I was thinking aloud a little, I confess. All this has come as a surprise.'

Playing for time, Ghote thought.

'Yes, sir,' he said blankly. 'And your movements at the time in question?'

Sir Rustomjee smiled his weary smile.

'You must allow me a few moments, Inspector,' he said. 'We ordinary people do not carry a list of our movements about in our heads in case we are questioned by the police, you know.'

'That is a common feeling, sir,' Ghote replied. 'But nevertheless if you begin thinking, it will very quickly come back to you.'

'Yes, no doubt.'

221

And then Sir Rustomjee shut his eyes.

Ghote experienced a quick spark of annoyance. It was typical of this sort of person. Very well, he had invited him to think. But calmly, and insolently, to shut his eyes in that fashion.

'Well, Sir Rustomjee?' he said sharply.

The eyes, below their heavy rampart of brow, opened suddenly.

'Yes,' Sir Rustomjee said. 'I was here, in this house. Probably in this room. No. No, not in this room.'

He had added the last few words with a sudden hurry. Ghote pounced.

'Not in this room? Why do you say that?'

'Because I was not in here, Inspector.'

The words were calm, studiedly calm. Ghote accepted a defeat.

'Then where were you, sir?' he asked stolidly.

'In my own room, Inspector.'

Sir Rustomjee leaned forward as if for emphasis.

'You may find it curious,' he said, 'that I should not have spent the evening in this well-furnished comfortable room in the house my family own.'

Ghote sat unmoving.

'Yes,' Sir Rustomjee went on, as Ghote had known he would. 'Yes, you might find that odd, at first sight. But it is perfectly simple really, Inspector. I have always tended to be a lone

222

bird, you know. I like to be on my own to think. And Homi is an excellent fellow, but he will chat.'

Ghote felt a creeping sense of disappointment. Was all that was worrying Sir Rustomjee merely the necessity to account for his not having spent the evening with his own brother when they were both in the same house? Some people could afford the luxury of fine feelings.

'So what you are telling,' he said, a little irritatedly, 'is that you spent the evening in your room, while your brother happened to be in here.'

'No. Oh, no.'

Sir Rustomjee sounded positively dismayed. What on earth was all this about? Again he waited for Sir Rustomjee to make matters worse.

'No, Inspector. We were both up in my room. That is what I have not sufficiently explained to you. The room is my bedroom, of course, but it is also, if you like, my private sitting-room. Chairs. Chairs, you know, and so forth.'

And now Sir Rustomjee was waiting for him.

'I see,' Ghote said. 'You and your brother spent the evening together up in your room?'

'Yes. Yes, exactly.'

Well, it was a perfectly good explanation, and Sir Rustomjee had provided himself with an excellent alibi.

Why then had he insisted on saying so much? Ghote decided he would not leave the loose-end dangling.

'But why was it, then,' he asked, 'that you did not both sit down here, in this most comfortable and delightful room, if you were happy on this occasion to listen to your brother chat?'

And Sir Rustomjee was positively nonplussed. He failed to answer for some time. He opened his mouth and said nothing. He licked along the edge of his top lip, almost furtively. At last he broke out in a sudden spasm of petulance.

'Really, Inspector. Cannot a man sit where he likes in his own home? We happened to spend the evening in my room. I told you there are chairs there. Chairs. Why should my brother and I not be in there as well as here?'

He stared challengingly at Ghote. And it was certainly a question which Ghote could not answer. Why not indeed? If you had a house with plenty of rooms in it, with chairs in them, then why should you not sit here and there as the fancy took you?

'No reason, no reason at all, Sir Rustomjee,' he said.

He stood up, feeling the light sweat that had sprung up down his back cooling with the sudden movement.

'Well, thank you, sir,' he said. 'You have

been most kind in answering all my questions. Most helpful. You realise, I hope, that they had to be asked?'

'Yes, yes, of course,' Sir Rustomjee replied, all affability now. 'And there is nothing more I can do for you? Nothing more I can tell you?'

'No, no,' Ghote said. 'No, I do not think so. Thank you.'

It was difficult to say which of them seemed more pleased that they were parting on friendly terms.

'Then I'll just see you out, my dear fellow,' Sir Rustomjee said.

He made for the door. But before he had got there it was quietly opened. The youngish, smart Goan bearer stood there.

'Excuse, sahib,' he said to Sir Rustomjee. 'There is a telephone call. For this gentleman.'

He inclined his head in Ghote's direction.

'A telephone call. Ah, yes. Yes,' said Sir Rustomjee.

He turned to Ghote.

'Well, I'll say good-bye, my dear fellow,' he said. 'Felix will show you where the phone is and all that.'

'Good-bye, Sir Rustomjee. And thank you again.'

Ghote followed the bearer out. He was led to another room on the ground floor, a smaller one than the shaded drawing-room, evidently some sort of a study to judge by the big old-fashioned roll-top desk that stood against one

225

wall. It was open, but the assorted papers on it looked dusty as if the room was little used. There were, however, three confortable-looking brown leather arm-chairs, Ghote noticed. If Sir Rustomjee had a fancy to sit somewhere else than in his drawing-room he had plenty of choice, it seemed.

On a curious shelved piece of furniture opposite the desk the telephone was standing with the receiver lying beside it. He picked it up and darted a look at Felix.

The bearer bowed slightly and went out.

Ghote picked up the receiver.

'Inspector Ghote speaking.'

It was Headquarters. A message from D.S.P. Naik. This was the duty sergeant.

'Yes? What is it, Sergeant?'

'The D.S.P. would like you to go out to Juhu Beach straight away, Inspector. A man called Lal Dass has been arrested there. A hathayogi. He is at Ville Parle police station.'

14

Ghote, driving along the wide road following the coast northwards at a fair speed, though nothing like as fast as he would have liked, wished he had been able to find out more about this arrest of Lal Dass. But the duty sergeant had been able to tell him practically nothing.

Leaving the select Breach Candy swimming baths behind to his left and approaching the highly unselect great bulk of the Mahalaxmi Temple, he asked himself: Why Juhu? What on earth was Lal Dass doing there? He had left him comfortably installed—no, highly uncomfortably—on the beach not far ahead of where he was now at Worli. It was a good six miles farther before you got to Juhu. Why had Lal Dass gone there? It was not as though the favourite sands of the wealthier Bombayites were the sort of place that the hathayogi would be at home in.

On the other hand you could never tell with a religious figure like that.

The main road took him a little inland at Worli at the point where he had had that unsatisfactory interview with Lal Dass crouching under that damned awning. Luckily there was less and less traffic with every half mile. He could begin to make some real progress.

Mahim and the long bridge across the creek to Sandra. Three miles to go now. He turned, feeling more cheerful, to state this obvious fact to Desai, sitting slumped and mercifully silent beside him.

Desai was asleep.

And at last, down to his left a glimpse of the enormous stretch of the sands through gaps between houses and beyond a fringe of tall palms. And now a turn right, and here was Ville Parle police station.

He left Desai where he was—guarding the truck, you could call it—and walked straight in.

'Ghote,' he said to the man at the desk. 'Inspector, C.I.D.'

The man's face broke into a smile, half simple greeting, and half something else which Ghote did not quite like. A touch maliceful, as if there was something decidedly amusing in the situation. But he was quick to point out the office Ghote wanted.

'Inspector Gadgil is waiting for you, Inspector.'

Gadgil. Ghote's heart sank. Was he involved in this too? Another encounter with the little swagger-stick flourishing figure who had locked poor ageing Captain Harbaksh Singh in the Rajah's lavatory was hardly welcome.

What would his attitude be now?

He knocked on the office door.

'Come. Come,' a voice barked out.

Wearily Ghote went in.

'Ah, Inspector, glad you could get here,' Gadgil said, bouncing up from behind a meticulously laid-out desk.

They shook hands.

So far so good, Ghote thought pessimistically.

'Well, Inspector,' he said, 'you will have to put me in the picture. I got the most short report from Headquarters only. I was out on an investigation.'

A peace offering of this sort might not come amiss.

Inspector Gadgil sat neatly back in his chair. The swagger-stick lay, precisely placed, on the desk in front of him near the front edge.

'Take a seat Inspector. Please take a seat,' he said.

Ghote sat on the battered little cane armchair he saw and waited.

'I made the arrest personally,' Inspector Gadgil began. 'I was informed by the constable making the routine patrol I had ordered that there was an intruder in the Rajah of Bhedwar—in the ex-Rajah of Bhedwar's bungalow.'

'In the bungalow?' Ghote said, unable to conceal his surprise.

'Yes, yes. I had given strict orders that a patrol was to inspect the building at intervals of not less than two hours. You get all sorts of unwelcome people about after a case like this, the Press, sightseers.'

Gadgil twitched his little black brush of a moustache with distaste.

'And your patrol reported Lal Dass was actually inside the shack?' Ghote said, with a hint of sharpness.

'In the back shed. In occupancy. And so of course I immediately went along there in person and effected the arrest.'

On a murder charge? Again? The thought appalled Ghote. Tentatively he set about discovering whether it was true.

'You arrested him and charged him?' he said.

'Yes. I brought in a charge of unlawful entry,' Gadgil replied.

He rubbed his hands together in front of him. The dry skin of his palms made a brisk rustling noise.

'But of course,' he added, 'that was only in the nature of a holding charge.'

'A holding charge?'

'I left it to you to make the formal charge of murder under Section 201.'

'Thank you,' Ghote said.

'Just as well for me not to get involved at the stage of giving evidence,' Gadgil replied. 'Plenty to do out here, you know, without having to spend days waiting to go into the box.'

'Did you—Did you ask Lal Dass what he was doing at the shack?' Ghote asked.

'Certainly not. That was hardly my province.'

'But it is mine?'

Ghote stood up.

'And I think,' he said, 'that I will go and carry it out.'

*   *   *

Lal Dass was sitting on the floor of the bare cell in what looked exactly the attitude he had sat in on the beach at Worli. He looked no different in any way. Even in the poor light coming through the tiny square of barred window high up in the far wall of the cell his skin could be seen to glisten smoothly. His face was uncreased by the slightest suspicion of a frown.

'Lal Dass,' Ghote began formally.

The hathayogi did look up.

'You will recall me,' Ghote said. 'I am Inspector Ghote of the Bombay C.I.D. and I am inquiring into the circumstances of the death of the Rajah of Bhedwar.'

Lal Dass's big, limpid eyes were on him though he did not speak.

'Earlier this evening,' Ghote said, 'you were found at the late Rajah's bungalow near here at Juhu Beach. Did you have any right to be there?'

'Yes,' said Lal Dass.

Ghote's head jerked forward in surprise.

'Yes? You did have a right to be there?'

'Yes,' said Lal Dass with unshakable composure. 'I did have right. It was you who gave me the right.'

For a quick moment Ghote thought. What on earth had he said that Lal Dass could have construed as giving him a right to enter that bungalow? He could think of nothing, and was reduced to asking.

'How did I give you that right?'

'You told the bungalow was empty. If the Rajah had no more use for it, it was there.'

Oh no, Ghote thought, you could not go about things in such a way.

Only you could. Human beings were capable of anything, any irresponsibility, any fantastic process of self-delusion.

'It was there empty,' he said, 'so you thought you would just stroll along and make yourself perfectly at home? Is that it? Have I got it quite right?'

'I was having difficulties,' Lal Dass said, in a tone that indicated this was a complete and satisfactory explanation.

'Difficulties? What sort of difficulties?'

It was no use doing anything other than just asking.

'I have my difficulties,' Lal Dass replied.

For once his air of bland composure seemed to have deserted him. He was no longer looking limpid-eyed at Ghote.

Ghote smelt the faintest hint of a trail.

'What were the nature of these difficulties?' he snapped. 'What you have told is not sufficient answer.'

Slowly Lal Dass's head sank till he was looking hard at the stained concrete floor of the cell.

'It was those boys,' he said in a whisper.

Ghote felt an inclination to burst into tears.

'What boys? What is this, for heaven's sake?'

Still Lal Dass regarded the brown floor.

'They were preventing me from perfecting myself,' he said. 'I was unable to fix my concentration. They were the boys I told about, the ones who would pull down my shade and they would throw stones also.'

Now Ghote did at least see what the odd logic of the situation was.

'Some boys stopped you meditating,' he said, allowing himself a little amusement. 'You, the famous hathayogi.'

Lal Dass seemed to react to the mockery. His head came swiftly up and he looked straight at Ghote standing in front of him.

'That is what I have told,' he said. 'That is what I told you before. I am far away from subduing my thoughts.'

He looked away. His simple shame-facedness made Ghote in his turn ashamed that he had, even if only a little, laughed at him.

'And that is not the whole,' Lal Dass added in a whisper again.

'There is more?' Ghote asked.

He squatted on his hunkers till he was more nearly at the hathayogi's level.

'I felt,' Lal Dass said, evidently encouraged, 'I felt that if I could have peace I would subdue not my thoughts only but my body also. I felt that then I could walk on the water.'

The words fell like hammer strokes on Ghote.

'You mean you still believe you can do that?' he asked. 'You intend to try once more?'

'Once more. Perhaps many times more. But when I know I am ready only.'

It was spoken with total assurance.

Ghote replied with scarcely any assurance at all.

'Then—then you do not regard your life as finished after that hoax?' he said.

'It was a small mistake,' Lal Dass replied. 'It was perhaps a good thing. After something like that I will not have people all round me. Before they did take away from the concentration. I know that.'

'Yes,' said Ghote. 'You will certainly hardly be surrounded by admirers now. And nor will you receive those admirers' food, and cash, and comforts.'

'No,' said Lal Dass.

He looked at Ghote once more, and in his limpid eyes there was the hint of spiritual shrewdness that Ghote had seen before on the beach.

'No,' Lal Dass said. 'But, if I had been talking of walking on water for food and cash only, I would not have been sitting there on the beach where you found me afterwards, would I?'

He gave Ghote a fleeting smile.

'You are a man of experience, Inspector,' he said. 'You must know that India is full of rogues who pretend to be religious. They are most of them too clever to be found out. But when they are, they do one thing quickly: they go just as fast as they can to somewhere where they are not known and they set up in business once more. India is a big country, Inspector.'

Ghote admitted defeat. He said nothing but rose, a little stiffly, from his crouching position.

'Well, Lal Dass,' he said, 'will spending a little time in prison stop your programme for subjugating your body?'

Lal Dass did look up at him with a hint of query in his mild eyes.

'Because that is almost certainly where you are going to go,' Ghote said. 'On a breaking and entering conviction. Inspector Gadgil will see to that.'

*   *   *

Inspector Gadgil did not take it kindly. But there was nothing he could do about it.

He came out with Ghote to the entrance to the station, darting a look of pettish ferocity at the unfortunate man at the cluttered desk.

'Get those things put away, Constable,' he snapped, turning aside from Ghote. 'How often have I told you a police station is not a section of the pavement for you to lay out your wares on?'

'No, sir. Yes, sir.'

Books and papers were hurriedly shoved

out of, sight beneath the counter. Inspector Gadgil turned back to Ghote.

'Sorry about that, Inspector. Vital to keep men up to the mark. And now, tell me, you are going to continue your inquiries elsewhere?'

Ghote reflected with bitterness that in a way Gadgil was entitled to be put in the picture. And he had had the shrewdness to ask his question where he would have to be snubbed in front of a subordinate if he was not to get a reply. Only what reply was there to give? That he was going to see 'a certain racehorse owner'? But he had no particular new evidence to put to Anil Bedekar. That he was going to put some questions to 'a well-known figure in the scientific field'? He had hardly left Sir Rustomjee as it was.

'Oh, yes, yes, Inspector,' he said to Gadgil. 'Plainly this development here warranted immediate attention. But on the other hand, my inquiries are taking—'

And then, mercifully, the most hideous row abruptly broke out on the steps leading into the building. Without appearing to dodge the issue in any way, he could reasonably break off and look to see what the matter was. Gadgil, in any case, was frowning like a little thundercloud and tapping his swagger-stick ominously against his calf.

He trotted off towards the pair of double swing doors. But, before he had reached them, they both swung back with a pair of sharp

236

clacks and two constables staggered through, each hanging on to one arm of an extremely drunken European.

Ghote saw, with decided alarm, that this was none other than Jack Cooper. The tubby little racehorse trainer was in a state of wildly noisy jollity. He stood in the entrance, forcing the two hefty constables who had hold of him to stay where they were, and he shouted.

'That's right, lads, lead me in. Lead on, Macduff. To gaol or victory. Jack Cooper won't mind which. Jack Cooper's got a real winner, and Jack's going to tell the world.'

Inspector Gadgil's mouth hardened like a little steel trap under the black brush of his moustache.

'Get that man down to the cells,' he barked.

'Yes, sir. Right away, Inspector.'

But Jack Cooper, with the perverse obstinacy of the very drunk, promptly took it into his head to continue his stand in the entrance way. He stopped shouting to bring his whole wavering concentration to bear on the problem of preventing the constables hauling him past the counter and down the short flight of stone steps to the police station's battery of eight cells.

And he happened to be in an excellent position to do so. The entrance way was a little too narrow for three people to go through it abreast and so neither of the constables could bring full pressure to bear. But Jack, by spreading his short arms as wide as possible and firmly planting his two tubby legs on the ground, was able to exert considerable force on both of them.

'Come on, come on.'

Inspector Gadgil's swagger-stick was beating a tattoo of frenzied impatience on his calf.

'The chap was creating a disturbance in the Sun 'n Sand Hotel, Inspector,' one of the hefty constables gasped out in intervals of the struggle, perhaps hoping that a little information would serve as a sop to his superior.

'I do not care where he was creating a disturbance,' Gadgil snapped. 'I will not have him making a nuisance of himself in my station.'

Jack Cooper, beetroot-faced and perspiring, evidently heard the words, for all the intensity of his struggle at the door. Because he promptly abandoned that stage in his fighting career and shot along the length of the counter till he was almost in front of Gadgil.

The two constables came slipping and sliding along willy-nilly behind him, still clutching hard at his podgy arms. Jack looked up at Gadgil, his intensely blue eyes alive with mischief.

'Ooh, dear, ooh dear, ooh dear,' he said in a comical high-pitched voice. 'Spoiling the quiet of your little station, are we? Tut, tut, tut, tut.

238

Mustn't do that, must we?'

Ghote, who had noticed Jack's change of tactics the moment he had shifted his stance in the doorway, edged quietly to one side.

Whatever happened, he did not want the little English racehorse trainer to notice him. If he chose to get drunk like this, then a night in the cells was the least he deserved.

Quietly he began edging along the far wall from the counter in the direction of the now clear doorway.

He had almost reached it and was taking a quiet look back, from a position comfortably behind the bouncy Jack Cooper, who was now engaged in singing a version of a lullaby to Inspector Gadgil, when the doors were flung wide open again and a dishevelled figure appeared at them shouting 'Inspector Ghote, Inspector Ghote.'

It was Sgt Desai. Of course. And the impact of his sudden dramatic arrival was enough to silence even Jack Cooper.

'Inspector Ghote. Where is Inspector Ghote?' Desai shouted.

'Here I am,' Ghote said, trying simultaneously to keep his voice down and yet to speak with enough force to attract Desai's attention.

And all he succeeded in doing, as he knew he would, was to attract Jack Cooper's attention.

'Why, it's me old pal, Inspector Ghote.

Ganesh Ghote to his friends. What a piece of luck. What a very, very lucky meeting.'

Still dragging the two bewildered constables, Jack Cooper progressed back towards the entrance and stopped in front of Ghote.

'Now, my dear old pal,' he said, 'there's a little something you can do for me.'

Ghote pretended to ignore him. He stepped smartly past the little white-haired, stocky aggressive figure and went up to Desai.

'Well, Sergeant,' he said sharply. 'What is it?'

'Inspector,' Desai answered, a radiant grin spreading itself all over his face. 'Inspector, I fell asleep in the truck and when I woke up you were gone. I thought you'd left without me.'

Ghote grinned, without mirth.

'Splendid,' he said. 'You are sitting in the truck which I use as transport. You wake up, and you wonder where I have gone. Where do you think I have gone without my truck, you idiot!'

To avoid witnessing the whole of the long look of dawning comprehension that began to work its way to the surface of Desai's visage, he turned away.

Only to come face to face with Jack Cooper again.

'My dear friend, my very, very dear friend. There is a little something you can do.'

Ghote could not avoid looking at him. The shock of white hair, so unbecoming on such an irresponsibly gay figure, the puce complexion assisted by years of alcoholic consumption, the bright, bright blue eyes, at times so disconcerting with their direct appraisal of other men's motives.

'Mr Cooper, good evening,' he said. 'But I am afraid I am in a great hurry. Police work, you know.'

He turned to move away.

'My dear friend, I know you don't want to have anything to do with an old reprobate like me. But these people are going to bung me in one of their filthy cells, you know. You can't let that happen to an old pal.'

Ghote turned back to him.

'Mr Cooper, I am not an old pal,' he said with controlled reasonableness. 'We have met twice only. And, to tell the truth, you are most disgracefully drunk. You should be put in a cell.'

The bright blue eyes in the beetroot face blinked once, sharply.

'I know I should, old pal. I am most disgracefully drunk. That gee-gee that was worrying me so got an absolutely clear bill of health from the old vet today. I had to celebrate.'

He shook his head mournfully, the pure white shock of hair moving.

'But all the same, old boy—old pal, no—all

241

the same, old boy, won't you do something for me?'

'But you know it is my duty to see that the law is upheld,' Ghote said.

Yet he realised that already he was weakening.

Jack Cooper must have seen it too, in spite of the efforts he made to keep his face unexpressive.

'My dear old pa—No.'

With immense solemnity he began again.

'My dear Inspector Ganesh Ghote. Sahib. I knew you would do it. I thank you. From the bottom of my heart.'

Resignedly Ghote turned to Inspector Gadgil.

'Inspector, as you have gathered, this is an acquaintance of mine. I would think you would be pleased not to have to deal with him?'

It was an appeal to which Gadgil did not exactly respond well. He pursed his lips under the little black brush of a moustache and tapped at the palm of his left hand with the tip of his swagger-stick.

'Very well, Inspector,' he said. 'I put him in your care. But against my better judgment, mind. Against my better judgment.'

'Thank you,' Ghote said.

He took Jack Cooper firmly by the elbow and steered him out of the double doors, giving Sgt Desai a vicious glare out of the corner of his eye as he did so. To his infinite relief Jack made no trouble as they went over to the truck and got in. Indeed, no sooner had Ghote started the engine than Jack, with a last 'Dear old pal,' closed his bright eyes and appeared to go straight off to sleep.

Ghote waited till they were on the road and then shook his shoulder.

'Do we take you back to the stables?' he said.

Jack Cooper hiccupped.

'Not at all,' he said. 'Little hotel. In Morton Road. The Lucky Welcome.'

He relapsed into silence. But evidently he was not asleep, because a moment later he added something.

'Little hotel,' he said. 'Beastly South Indian food. And you know where the boss man stays when we come to Bombay together like this? The Taj. No less. The jolly old Taj Mahal Hotel, built all bloody well back to front.'

Again silence except for groany breathing, audible even above the noise of the engine. And then again another unsolicited remark.

'That's where they all stay, my friends. My jolly old friends. That's where they're all pals together. The jolly old Taj. My old boss man, your young Rajah. Pals.'

Abruptly Ghote felt a waft of whisky breath all over him. Jack Cooper had suddenly hauled himself upright.

'But that doesn't stop friendly old boss man putting nasty little private detective on to trailing friendly young Rajah, member of the House of Princes, God bless 'em all.'

And after that total silence and the merciful withdrawal of the whisky breath.

In the darkness of the driving cab, with the slumped figure of the English trainer a vague whitish blur beside him and with Desai in the back humming another of his interminable film tunes, Ghote was able to sit quietly and savour the piece of information that had been so oddly thrown into his lap.

So Anil Bedekar had hired a private detective to follow the Rajah of Bhedwar, had he? To follow the man he in no way suspected of being the joker who had played that notorious trick on him on the day of the last Indian Derby? Now he knew whom he was going to see next.

15

Ghote left Desai outside the Lucky Welcome Hotel in Morton Road, a tattered building in a tattered street, with Jack Cooper's arm round his shoulders. Jack was still half-asleep and it was a question whether he thought he was being supported by Ghote himself. He lolled forward, with his pot-belly looming out in a wide curve of blotchy whiteness in the shadowed darkness of the street.

Ghote left them there, heartlessly.

And then he drove himself quietly and quickly to the huge minaretted block of the Taj Mahal Hotel, a great rectangle of shining pinpoint lights beside the dark waters of the harbour at the Gateway of India. He felt, with the abandonment of the two burdensome figures that he had been saddled with—one as the result of D.S.P. Naik's altogether uncharacteristic irresponsibility, the other as a pure visitation from the wanton spirit of chance—a new sense of calm confidence. He had just come into possession, never mind how, of a simple, solid piece of information in a case which, thanks to the Rajah's utter detachment from everything, had up till now almost completely lacked anything to get the teeth into.

But now he had caught out Anil Bedekar in a plain piece of lying about his relations with the murdered man. Now had come the moment of plain truth.

He entered the big, grand-looking, marble-floored foyer of the luxurious hotel, with its little brightly-lit, glossy boutiques all round, its chattering ticker-tape machine plaything of the rich—and its constantly coming and going well-clad people, a changing pattern of richly coloured silky saris, frosty white suits, the occasional discreet black of a dinner jacket. His mouth set in a grim line.

The enormously tall Pathan hall porter

advanced towards him.

'C.I.D.,' Ghote said sharply, deliberately speaking just loudly enough to give the man the heebie-jeebies that such an unspeakable word in these surroundings might just have been caught by the casual ears.

'You would want the manager, Superintendent sahib?' the doorman asked, inclining from his great height towards Ghote.

'I wish to see Mr Anil Bedekar,' Ghote said. 'I am Inspector Ganesh Ghote.'

'Very well, sahib. If you would be so good as to wait.'

The hall porter cast a swift glance round over the heads of the people coming and going, as if first to spot somewhere he could tuck this unwelcome visitor away, and second to find a bearer to get hold of Anil Bedekar as quickly as possible.

He found the bearer first, summoned him to his side with a glance of fire, issued him with instructions in a voice so low that Ghote himself, standing just beside them, could not hear, and sent him on his way at full, discreet speed.

The instructions must have been very terse. In less than a minute and a half the bearer was back. A whispered word to the porter. The porter leant towards Ghote again.

'Mr Bedekar is out on the terrace, Inspector sahib. He is alone. He would see you there.'

The way in which he dropped his voice on

the word 'Inspector' while still actually pronouncing it was eloquent testimony to the qualities which kept him in the job. Ghote took pleasure in not offering him a tip at the public expense. He followed the bearer, marching through the great dining-room with its tables covered in dense white cloths and heavy silvery cutlery, with its army of alert waiters ready to dart forward at the least behest of any of the remaining later diners, and out into the soft darkness of the broad terrace.

Out here too there were tables, and at some of them people were sitting, the white glimmer of coffee cups in front of them and the translucent glint of glasses. Beyond, the harbour spread out into the night with the Dolphin Light breaking out intermittently away towards the right and other smaller glints flicking here and there or progressing at infinitely slow speed across the faintly glinting black surface of the calm water.

The bearer led him to a small table at the far end of the wide terrace where Anil Bedekar sat alone at a little distance from the nearest other diners. In front of him, too, there was the luxurious apparatus of coffee-drinking in these surroundings, of which the little white cup on the edge of the round table seemed the least significant part.

He looked up at the soft-footed approach of the bearer.

'Inspector, Inspector,' he said bonhomously as he saw Ghote. 'What is it I can do for you? You will drink some coffee? Bearer, another cup.'

'No. No coffee,' Ghote said sharply.

Anil Bedekar looked at Ghote, standing stiffly above him.

'Come, sit, sit, Inspector,' he said.

Ghote pulled the second chair away from the table, placed it exactly at right angles to Anil Bedekar's and sat down on it. At attention.

The racehorse-owner stretched both arms high above his head, the fiery-tipped cigar standing out like a beacon.

'This is the end of a good day for me,' he said.

He flicked his head round and gave Ghote a shrewd glance.

'You know nothing about horseracing, Inspector?' he said, both statement and question.

'I know very little,' Ghote conceded, with grudgingness.

'Then you would find it hard to tell how I am feeling.'

Slowly and luxuriatingly Anil Bedekar brought his two arms down from their outstretched position. Ghote was unable to prevent a little pulling-down, disapproving motion at the corners of his mouth.

'Yes,' he answered. 'I imagine I would find it

very difficult.'

A crooked grin creased Bedekar's monkey-face like a streak of forked lightning.

'You disapprove of the racing game, my Inspector,' he said. 'You think it is all a waste and a wicked way to spend your life.'

Ghote made no reply. Which was in fact pointedly to omit the necessary denial.

'And yet,' Anil Bedekar went on, blowing out the cigar smoke now in a long funnel of aromatic greyness. 'And yet my useless hobby is not such a bad thing, you know.'

Suddenly he crouched forward across the table and looked straight into Ghote's eyes.

'If five other poor boys in Bombay had wanted to win the Indian Derby as much as I did,' he said, 'then there would be five hundred fewer people sleeping on the pavements of the city now. Five hundred and five.'

Ghote thought about it. Perhaps it was true. The energy this man had shown in his single-minded pursuit of the intangible thing that was a winning horse in the Indian Derby was after all what India needed, so they said. Five times that energy would have added a good deal to the wealth of this city, have seeped down to those pavement sleepers.

His train of acquiescence must have shown itself a little on his features: Anil Bedekar laughed again, a laugh of rich enjoyment.

'Now, tell me, Inspector,' he said with

249

abrupt briskness, 'what is it you have come for?'

Ghote straightened his back in the woven cane chair.

'Mr Bedekar,' he said with formality, 'I am inquiring into the death of the Rajah of Bhedwar.'

Anil Bedekar tapped the ash from his cigar into the big, round ash-tray.

'A sad business,' he said, 'a sad business.'

But he did not sound sad. He sounded as if he was enjoying life so much that a little wise nodding over someone else's misfortune was being shot through the heart.

'Mr Bedekar, when I put certain questions to you early this morning, you told you had no suspicions that the late Rajah was responsible for a series of practical jokes of which one was the substituting for your horse Roadside Romeo of a donkey shortly before the said horse was due to run in the Indian Derby.'

'Yes, yes, I told.'

A long deep inhalation from the cigar.

'And do you now repeat that you never suspected this?'

Anil Bedekar's eyes above the glowing point of the cigar were narrowed and shrewd. But he showed no sign of anxiety.

'Yes, yes,' he said, mumblingly round the cigar end, 'no suspicions I had. But you still say he did those things?'

'Most certainly I do,' Ghote said, picking his

250

words with double care. 'He was responsible for a series of major practical jokes, and because of them he was murdered. He had not ties. He had no one to hate him, except for those people in the last few months he had chosen to play his jokes upon.'

The big cigar waved lazily again.

'If you say, if you say.'

'And you were one of his victims.'

'You seem to be very certain, Inspector. I suppose you are right.'

'But you never suspected him?'

'I have told. I never suspected.'

An edge of irritation now.

Ghote pounced.

'Then why did you have the late Rajah followed?' Anil Bedekar leant back in his chair and laughed.

'Oh, Inspector.'

But he could not go on, he was laughing so much.

'Oh, Inspector,' he gasped out at last. 'And because of this you suspected me?'

Ghote held his face rigid.

'It is a circumstance that must be explained,' he said. 'And so far you have offered no explanation.'

Bedekar wiped tears from his eyes with the hairy back of his hard little hand.

'Yes, you are right,' he said. 'It was foolish of me. I should have told. I should have told you I had had this done this morning. Then I thought that, if I mentioned, perhaps you would not understand.'

He leant forward earnestly.

'This morning,' he said, 'at first I was not thinking very clearly. I was thinking about other things when you were talking. And that is a mistake.'

Ghote waited in silence for him to continue.

'Yes,' the racehorse-owner said reflectively, 'I should have told then. Now it is going to sound even less convincing.'

'It will have to be convincing,' Ghote said, allowing himself a ration of grimness. 'Otherwise I will not remain convinced there is insufficient evidence to arrest you on a charge of murder.'

But the threat simply replaced the twinkle in Anil Bedekar's sharp eyes.

'Well?' Ghote snapped.

Anil Bedekar sighed.

'I had Bunny Baindur followed,' he said, 'for a simple reason only: suddenly one day he began to ask questions about the running of my stables.'

He gave a grunt of a laugh.

'Oh,' he said, 'he thought he was being very clever and that I had noticed nothing. But Anil Bedekar is not so easy to fool. I had noticed, though I did not let him see that I had. And then as soon as he had left me I put on to him a private detective I use sometimes.'

'Yes,' said Ghote. 'The Rajah asked

questions about your horses. You put a detective on to him. You found he was responsible for that trick that made you the laughing stock of the whole racing world.'

Anil Bedekar waved it all away with the fiery red tip of his plump cigar.

'I could not have found he had changed Roadside Romeo into a donkey,' he said, 'because at that time he had not done anything of the sort. Ask my detective. No, I see now that this is what he was planning to do, but at the time I thought only he was intending to nobble one of my runners.'

'To nobble?' Ghote said.

A flash of impatience came into the racehorse-owner's eyes.

'I thought he intended to spoil the running of one of my horses so that he could put a big bet on something it would have beaten and made a packet,' he said. 'And as soon as I found that he did not need to make any packets I dropped the whole thing.'

'You found that he was a wealthy man?'

'Yes, yes. He looked like it always. But you can never tell. That I have learnt. But my man found it was so: he had a big income, though it died with him.'

'Yes, that is so,' Ghote conceded. 'But after the donkey incident had occurred, why did you not realise that that is what his plan had been?'

He looked hard at the squat little racehorse-owner.

Anil Bedekar shrugged.

'At first I was too angry, I suppose,' he said. 'I see that my account to you was not one hundred per cent convincing.'

'All right. At first you were too angry. But then?'

'Then something happened.'

A look of intense pleasure, concealed only to make it yet more delightful, crossed Bedekar's face.

'What happened?' Ghote asked angrily.

'You said you did not know much about racehorses?'

'Yes, yes.'

'Well,' Anil Bedekar said lazily, 'they are funny animals. Very funny. You know what happens to one of them sometimes, just out of the blue for no reason at all?'

'No.'

'Suddenly they change from being an ordinary sort of colt or filly into being a Number One top-notcher. Just like that. For no reason. It does not happen very often. But it can happen. Do not trust me for that. Ask anyone you like. Ask Jack Cooper.'

'And this has something to do with your explanation?' Ghote asked.

'Certainy, a lot to do with it. Because, you see, this thing happened to one of my colts, the one you saw this morning, Malvolio. I bought him because he was a fairly good looking horse and a bargain. I expected him to win a race

254

or two, but nothing much. And then this happened. Out at exercise he began to show fantastic form. We made a few quiet tests, ran a few gallops very early in the morning. And then I knew: I had got myself a cert for the Derby again. A real cert.'

Ghote looked at him levelly.

'And yet this morning you were a very worried man,' he said.

Anil Bedekar shrugged.

'I was a worried man. Yes. Not very worried, but worried. Malvolio had developed some fetlock trouble. It could have turned serious. But you saw how well he exercised this morning, and later the vet came and gave a most thorough examination. There is nothing at all wrong with that horse, Inspector. He is a champion of champions.'

'He will win the Indian Derby next year'?'

'It is as certain as anything ever was. I know it. I have known it for months now.'

He leant forward and stubbed out his half-smoked cigar.

'I knew it long before the Rajah was shot, Inspector,' he said.

16

Leaving the Taj Mahal Hotel, its foyer still full of elegant sari-clad women and well-dressed, paunchy men, and the dazzlingly bright rectangles of its little boutiques still glowing with lavishly displayed jewels, moulded and formed pottery and glitteringly embroidered cloths, Ghote soberly stated to himself that his case was not at an end.

A promising trail had been abruptly terminated. But things were no worse than that. Indeed Anil Bedekar's revelation simply meant that the affair had been solved a different way, by the process of elimination. Of the people the Rajah had confessed to hoaxing, there was now only Sir Rustomjee Currimbhoy left.

And, as soon as the figure of the old Parsi scientist came clearly into the forefront of his mind, Ghote realised something which, he saw, he ought to have noted long before. In his last interview with Sir Rustomjee one passage had stuck awkwardly out: the odd business of Sir Rustomjee's tiresome explanations about his choosing to spend the evening in his bedroom.

Ghote saw now, quite suddenly and clearly, why the old man had done this. Simply because this was the sole room in the house where it was reasonably likely that he would be free from observation by his own servants. A place where he could set himself up an alibi by pretending that at the time Bunny Baindur was shot his brother Homi had been there with him.

Ghote stopped in his tracks. He had been about to pay an unexpected visit on Sir

Rustomjee. Instead he turned back into the huge hotel and sought out a telephone.

The phone up at the Currimbhoy house was answered with promptness. Ghote recognised the voice of Felix, the Goan bearer. He asked, not for Sir Rustomjee, but for Mr Homi Currimbhoy.

There was a pause. Then Felix came back to the phone. 'Mr. Homi is not in, Inspector. I understand he is at his club. If you would care to call him there?'

Ghote said that he would. He asked for and was told the name of the club. He left the telephone and made straight for his truck.

He had not long to wait at the club before a bearer, in white with white turban and a broad red sash across one shoulder with his number on it in brass, came to tell him that Mr Currimbhoy was in the billiard room and would see him there. He followed the man through big, echoing corridors with well-polished woodblock floors, and was left at the opened door of the billiard room with a deferential salaam.

He looked in. The whole large room was deserted except for the single figure of Homi Currimbhoy. He was leaning over the edge of the farthest of the three big billiard tables, the only one with its long overhanging gold-fringed light-shade lit up. This light was in fact all the illumination the big room had, and Ghote could make out little of it, except that there was certainly no one else there, only dimly-seen racks with dozens of billiard cues of various lengths standing up in them like the bars of small cells, two or three sofas in dark wood with cane seats and a large glass-fronted cupboard high up on one wall inside which there could just be made out the full-bellied shapes of a number of silver cups and trophies.

From the lit table there came the soft double plock of one of the balls striking the other two.

'Ah,' said Homi Currimbhoy quietly to himself, 'neat, very neat, and that makes three hundred and twelve.'

Ghote cleared his throat a little. The rasping sound echoed very clearly in the cathedral quiet of the big high-ceilinged room.

'Just two moments if you don't mind,' Homi Currimbhoy said, without turning from the great area of lustrous green baize in front of him. 'Highly interesting little situation here.'

Again there came the soft double plock, and Homi, humming a little to himself, manoeuvred his way round the big table. Ghote watched in silence. He saw the long, dark cue slide slowly backwards and then shoot smoothly forward. Plock.

And silence. Nothing more.

'Bother,' said Homi Currimbhoy.

He straightened from the table and came across.

They sat down side by side on one of the

258

cane-seated sofas.

'Well now?' said Homi Currimbhoy.

'It is a matter concerning the night the Rajah of Bhedwar was shot, the night of the April seventh last.'

Homi Currimbhoy pulled a long face.

'Oh,' he said, 'but you shouldn't be asking me about that.'

'And why not?'

'Because I don't know a thing about it, old boy. Not a thing.'

He chuckled suddenly.

'Unless you think I killed the poor chap,' he added. Ghote looked at him blank-faced.

'I would like to know,' he said, 'where you were on the night of the seventh last between the hours of 8 p.m. and midnight.'

Homi Currimbhoy blinked.

'But I say,' he exclaimed. 'But really, old man. I mean, why?'

'In connection with inquiries,' Ghote replied primly.

The Parsi looked at him.

'Well,' he said, 'but all the same. I mean, stealing a bit of a cheeky run, aren't you?'

'There are questions it is my duty to ask.'

'Oh, I see.'

Homi pulled his face into a fittingly serious expression.

'Yes,' he said. 'Well then, I shall have to think.'

He fell silent.

'Not that, if I did get it wrong, it would really matter in the end,' he said. 'I mean, I didn't kill poor old Bunny, you know.'

'Please,' Ghote said, 'would you make every effort to be absolutely correct? What you tell may affect another person.'

Homi turned aside and resumed his thinking.

'Yes,' he said after a due interval. 'All clear in my mind now.'

'Well?'

'Yes. Well, at the time you mention I was— Wait a moment.'

Ghote found he was leaning forward with quivering anxiety.

'What?' he barked out.

'I think I know who you must have in mind.'

'Have in mind?'

'Yes. The fellow you think I should be giving an alibi to. I think it must be Rustomjee.'

He cocked an eye at Ghote. Ghote sat keeping his face rigidly uninformative.

'Hah,' said Homi, 'I see it is. Must be. Otherwise you'd have been bound to say "No".'

He drew in a deep breath.

'Well,' he said, 'let me tell you I think you've hardly been playing cricket. I mean, to try and trap a fellow into betraying his own brother. Not good enough, you know. Simply not good enough.'

'I am not playing cricket,' Ghote burst out.

260

'I am investigating a murder. Where were you on the night of the seventh last?'

The big billiard room was very quiet. The light beat down from the long fringed shade over the green, green table. The three balls that Homi had been playing with lay poised where he had left them, the two white and the startling red.

'I spent the whole evening at the house,' Homi said. 'I've worked out that it must be so, because that was the night of the Cricket Club of India dinner, and at the last minute I couldn't go because I had a beastly attack of billiousness.'

'And so you stayed in?'

'Yes.'

'What exactly did you do?'

'Do?'

Homi thought.

'Well,' he said, 'I pottered about.'

'You pottered about? Does that mean you went here and there about the house?'

Homi lifted his head in a slight gesture of disapproval.

'Well, really,' he said. 'I mean "pottered about" means "pottered about". I don't know exactly what it means. Why do you have to ask such extraordinary questions?'

Ghote tried again.

'But it would not mean you spent the whole time in one place, one particular part of the house?' he said.

'Oh, good gracious me, no. Whatever made you think I would do that? You can't know me very well, if you say that. No, I'm famous for never sticking at things. Always leaving one thing off and starting another. Might have been a much better cricketer if I'd just kept at it, you know: But there was always so much else to do—shikar, tennis. And I used to ride a good deal. Pity I was like that in a way. Still I enjoyed myself, and that's more than a lot of people can say. Look at old Rustomjee, for instance.'

Ghote grabbed at the invitation. Every scrap of information he could collect about the man whose alibi for murder had just been so casually knocked to pieces might help him now when it came to bringing the case to court.

'Your brother is very different from you?' he prompted.

'Oh, good lord, yes. Chalk and cheese, you know. Chalk and cheese.'

Homi Currimbhoy pushed himself up from the cane-seated sofa.

'But of course,' he said, 'when I say that Rustomjee was unhappy and I was happy that isn't altogether the truth. I mean, Rustomjee was happy too, in a way. In his way. Rather a sort of unhappy way, if you take my meaning.'

'Yes?' Ghote said.

'Yes. Well, I mean, he enjoyed working away night and day on his infernal machine. That's what I used to call it, you know. His infernal machine. Sort of joke.'

'Yes, I see.'

'Good, good. Well now, I'll tell you a funny thing.'

'Yes?'

Homi had padded across and fetched himself a billiard cue, a short light-coloured one this time. But now he came back and leaning on the cue with its butt by his feet, he addressed Ghote squarely.

'I'll tell you a funny thing: you might have thought that Rustomjee would really be unhappy when he had his work taken away from him by that wretched Bunny Baindur. He told the that you'd found out about that, by the way. Good work.'

Ghote frowned a little. It was not easy to follow Homi's thought processes.

'You were saying?' he asked.

'Saying? Was I? Oh, yes. 'Course I was. About Rustomjee. Well, you might have thought—Hey, wait a minute.'

Homi grasped the thin end of the stubby billiard cue with both hands and gripped at it as if he could squeeze in a fine jet from its tip a thought that eluded him.

'Yes,' he said. 'I see it all now.'

He smiled.

'I see what you've been after, Inspector. You thought that I—No, wait a moment. Yes. You either expected, or did not expect, me to give Rustomjee an alibi. To say I spent the evening

263

with him shut up in his room, the way he often is with that infernal gramophone of his. You expected that, or you did not, and when I said I hadn't, you thought old Rustomjee was the murderer. But, you see, he isn't. He only said I was with him because the dear old chap had taken it into his head that I had killed young Bunny because of the awful thing that Bunny had done to him.'

Suddenly he swung the billiard cue round till it was parallel with the floor and grasped it at either end. Then he began swinging it violently up and down horizontally in the agitation of trying to express himself.

'And that's just where I'd got to,' he said. 'About Rustomjee. You see, the odd thing is: he wasn't really all that unhappy about his work coming to an end. He was deeply hurt by it all at first, of course. But, really, that only lasted about a day. I could tell, you know, because after about a day he started to play his gramophone, and I knew that he wouldn't do that if he was unhappy. He loves music too much, you see?'

His eyes positively shone with the effort of putting his point across.

'And now we come to it,' he went on. 'You see, if I knew he hadn't really been made deeply unhappy by what Bunny had done, I wouldn't have any reason to kill Bunny, would I? And neither, of course, would Rustomjee. He was a bit sad, you know, because I think all that business sort of made him admit what he must have in a way realised years ago: that his research was never going to get him anywhere. He'd been frightfully brilliant, you know, at Cambridge and so forth. But he'd just gone off on a wrong track somewhere years and years ago, and had never been able to admit it. Much too old to start something new now, you see. Lacked the energy. Oh, dear me, yes.'

Slowly the billiard cue was lowered till it came to rest against the front of Homi's thighs. The explanation was over.

*　　　*　　　*

Weighed leadenly down, Ghote plodded back to the truck. This was the end. All his fine phrases about the Rajah being too much a free agent to have enemies and consequently having to be the victim of one of those he had so outrageously tricked had fallen to fragments around him. None of those he had tricked had wanted to revenge themselves.

He had frittered about with absurd notions and a murderer had got away with it.

Suddenly, as he neared the truck parked at a kerb behind Homi Currimbhoy's club, he stopped short.

No, it was too much.

Sgt Desai was there. He was sitting happily on the truck's running board and beside him there was as ugly and dirty a street boy as

265

could be seen in all Bombay. And the two of them were contentedly playing cards together. A greasy, battered-edged pack was laid out on the pavement between them and they were immersed in a game.

The bloody cheek.

Ghote strode forward. His shadow, cast by a nearby street lamp, shot out ahead of him like an avenging spirit. Its top passed over the array of cards. Desai looked up. Ghote fixed his features in a glare of blasting fury. Desai blinked dazedly, plainly failed to recognise him, lowered his head and returned in complete absorption to the game.

Ghote stood there, about three yards away, petrified in sheer amazement. The boy, who had looked up at the same moment as the sergeant and had clearly been ready to dart off the second this stranger looked as if he was going to act, now, in face of this immobility, also went back to the cards.

Ghote simply watched them play. He was too astonished to do anything else.

And slowly he began to take in details of the game. From his position above the two squatting players he was able to see both their hands as well as the cards laid out on the grimy surface of the pavement. And quite soon he was able to appreciate the state of play.

Poor Desai, as was only to be expected, had got himself into a really tight corner. He was well down, and had but one hope in his hand of getting out of trouble. This was to find a fourth for the three jacks, which were the only cards of any merit he held. And the fourth jack was securely in the boy's hand. Ghote stood and waited for the inevitable.

And then Desai drew another card from the small remaining face-down stack. Ghote leant forward, blinking, to peer at it in the pale light of the street-lamp. What on earth—Suddenly he realised. It was a joker. They were playing with a pack with a joker in it.

Desai rapidly laid down his three jacks with the joker making the fourth. The urchin gave a wry grin of disgust and the few tiny coins lying beside the cards on the pavement were divided almost equally.

'And I think that will do, Sergeant,' Ghote said loudly.

Desai leapt into the air, his features pathetically ready for the stinging reprimand. But Ghote simply grinned at him. After all, he had solved his mystery.

17

Looking back at it all afterwards, Ghote did not like to admit even to himself just how curious the mental process had been which had led him so abruptly to the one inevitable conclusion. But the process had really been simple enough. He had seen a joker in a pack of cards. His mind had given a sort of convulsive, twisted leap and he had started to look for a joker in his own particular blocked situation. And of course there had been one there, staring at him in the face.

He had gone round and got into the truck. The silent, abashed Desai had scrambled in on the other side. The street boy had vanished into the night. And Ghote had sat for a few minutes, ten at the most, working out details of times and circumstances.

Then he had been ready.

'Where are we going, Inspector?' Desai had asked in a scared voice as Ghote abruptly started the engine.

'Back to the office for two minutes first,' Ghote had answered with deliberate mystification.

So back to the office and a hasty search through the drawer in his desk where he 'filed' all those odd pieces of paper and information which he felt a vague obligation to keep but could never really think what to do with.

After a while he found what he had been looking for. It was a smart, printed sheet from the Ministry of Police Affairs and the Arts. It announced a new appointment at the Ministry. It had been decided, it said, that the Minister should have a Public Relations Officer. And at the bottom of the sheet it had mentioned that this office would be on call day and night out of office hours at a certain address. The document was signed by the new appointee himself. Ram Kamdar.

Ghote noted the address.

It was a flat in Cumballa Hill, a new block from the sound of it. Ghote drove there at top speed. There was a niggle of irrational fear somewhere inside him mockingly repeating that for some unaccountable reason, now that he at last knew what it was all about, he would somehow be too late.

With open-mouthed Desai trailing along behind him, he rang at the bell of the flat's newly-painted front door and was admitted by Ram Kamdar himself, sleek-suited and heavy-spectacled.

'My dear Satish,' the P.R.O. said, producing a wide smile, 'what can I do for you?'

'A few quick questions,' Ghote answered.

He decided not to attempt to correct the error over his first name.

'But, yes, old boy. That's what I say: a P.R.O. is on duty twenty-four hours a day.'

'Yes,' said Ghote. 'That is a point I wished to mention.'

Ram Kamdar's plumpish, shave-needing face looked blank.

'But come in, come in. I'm all alone,' he said. 'Company is welcome.'

He retreated in front of Ghote and Desai into the living-room of the flat. Ghote gave it a quick, half-curious glance. It was very new-looking and very up-to-date from the ebony-black hi-fi gramophone in one corner to the neatly recessed coloured book-shelves, empty of books, facing it. Ghote at once began to feel that he had somehow stepped into a magazine advertisement. He brushed at the front of his trousers, which in the course of the long, long day had become considerably creased.

Ram Kamdar gestured towards two of the light-wood, colourful latex-foam cushioned chairs.

'Sit down, gentlemen, sit down,' he said.

He moved to pick up a heavy square-cut smoked-glass decanter from a big, low, round table in the same light wood as the chairs.

'I do not think it will be necessary to sit,' Ghote said. 'This should not take many minutes.'

Ram Kamdar darted him a look of sharp curiosity.

'Well, what's it all about?' he said.

'You were saying you were on duty twenty-four hours a day,' Ghote answered.

'Yes, yes. I am at your service.'

'No, it is not that. It is just that I do truly believe you think and sleep and eat your job every hour that there is.'

Ram Kamdar shrugged his well-padded shoulders a little.

'We've got to create a climate of acceptance for the P.R.O. in today's India,' he said. 'It's a one hundred per cent task.'

'No,' said Ghote.

'No? What the hell do you mean?'

A harsh flush rose up on the heavy cheeks.

'That is where you are wrong,' Ghote said. 'That is where you went wrong altogether. No man must ever devote every bit of himself and his time to one thing. If he does so he becomes totally serious.'

'And what's wrong with that, my friend?' Ram Kamdar demanded on a plain note of aggression.

'Just that I am looking for a totally serious man when I am looking for a murderer,' Ghote replied. 'The murderer, unless he kills almost by accident, is someone who has gone past the ordinary human restraints. He is totally devoted to something. Just as you, Mr Kamdar, are so totally devoted to your P.R.O. mission that, when the Ministry it was your job to give a good image to was in danger of becoming a laughing-stock with your new Minister's pet flamingoes being shot dead one by one, it was too much for you, especially with your family connection with the former Minister. So when you found out who that joker was and saw he had not been arrested, you decided to stop him at all costs yourself.'

Ram Kamdar grinned frenziedly.

'You've got it all wrong, my friend,' he said. 'I never learnt the Rajah was the joker in question till after he was dead. You yourself told me in my office. You must remember.'

'I remember most clearly,' Ghote answered. 'And I remembered also most clearly a few minutes ago that you went to great lengths to hammer home the point that you did not know about the Rajah. I ought to have deduced something from it at the time.'

'And what was that?' Kamdar said with truculence.

'That you knew the Rajah was the joker much earlier.'

'What nonsense. How could I have known earlier?'

'It is quite simple,' Ghote said. 'You were with me when the Rajah telephoned and I indicated to him I knew he was the joker. You must have heard enough though you did not say a word about it.'

It was then that the almost lunatic Kamdar made his spring for freedom. Ghote was ready for some such move, but the sheer ferocity of the leap took him by surprise and he was flung to the ground, his fingers clutching scrabblingly at the sleek silkiness of Kamdar's jacket.

And so it was Desai who eventually sat, hard and firmly, on the Rajah of Bhedwar's murderer, just as he had sat on the squinting man in Anil Bedekar's stables, and brought the matter to a conclusion.

*　　*　　*

272

Later that night, however, as Ghote wearily made his way out of the Headquarters building after seeing to all the trail of formalities that came dragging after Kamdar's arrest, something more did happen.

'Ah, Inspector Ghote. Just the man.'

It was D.S.P. Naik, calling from behind him. He turned round resignedly.

'Yes, D.S.P. ?'

'I wanted to see you earlier but you were out, and then I have had to go to this damned dinner.'

D.S.P. Naik passed a hand across his lips which seemed to be a little greasy.

'What can I do for you, sir?'

'Just a small thing. I was talking earlier today to that excellent chappie, Ram Kamdar, the Minister's P.R.O., you know. Going to go far, mark my words.'

Complete icy numbness entered Ghote. He was too tired, too utterly exhausted to find any tactful way round. And the D.S.P. was going happily on.

'Yes, Ram Kamdar. Hm. Well, he told me the Ministry needed a Security Officer. Important job, in its way. And straightaway I thought of that fellow of yours.'

'Fellow of mine, D.S.P. ?'

Ghote's brain was numb.

'Yes, your sergeant. What's his name—er—Desai.'

'Oh, Desai, yes.'

And a sudden shaft of bright illumination.

'Why, yes, D.S.P. You are perfectly right, sir. Desai would be just the man for a job like that.'

'Thought so. Thought so.'

Stumbling out of the building, Ghote dazedly asked himself two bewildering questions. Had D.S.P. Naik winked at him, actually winked? And, worse, had he winked back?